BOYS of '59

R.J. Burroughs

Martin Sisters Publishing

Published by

Martin Sisters Publishing, LLC

www. martinsisterspublishing. com

Copyright © 2013 R.J. Burroughs

All rights reserved. Published in the United States by
Martin Sisters Publishing, LLC, Kentucky.
ISBN: 9781-62553-015-8
Fiction/Humor
Printed in the United States of America
Martin Sisters Publishing, LLC

I attended Verden Public Schools from first grade to third grade. I used Verden as the setting for my novels because it is where my grandmother lived. I lived with her during 1958, 1959 and 1960. I will always have a soft spot for Verden. I thought it would be great to have the students from Verden create the art for the front cover for The Boys of '59, this volume in my Boys series.

It went so well I plan to hold a cover contest as each new book in the Boys series is released.

Although the characters in my books are all fiction, the town is real, and, yes, there is still that little jail at the end of Main Street.

If you ever get a chance to visit Verden, Oklahoma do so, as the folks in town have lots of stories to tell, please believe me your life will change forever if you have the chance to drive down Main Street, and of course visit the old jail.

~ R.J. Burroughs

About the cover and title page artwork:

Book Cover Art by:
Alexis C. Brown
Age: 16, Grade 11, or Junior
Verden High School
Medium: Colored Pencil
2nd year art student
Art Teacher: Susan McCaughtry

Title Page Art by:
Austin H. Patterson
Age: 16, Grade 11, or Junior
Verden High School
Canadian Valley Tech Student
Medium: Colored Pencil
2nd year art student

DEDICATION

To all the Staff Members and Students of Verden School System, past and present.

Thanks for all your help; I plan to take this one a very long way.

Chapter One

This was the day the boys had been waiting for all year: the start of another summer vacation.

Three complete months, no school, sleep late, stay up late, do just about anything they wanted as long as they stayed out of trouble, or at least tried their very best to stay out of trouble. Staying out of trouble wasn't what they were best at, however they all seemed to have the knack at getting out of it.

One afternoon, walking back into school after playing softball workup during recess, Charlie said, "You know guys, I think even if we could all move in with them nuns living in Chickasha, and pray all day and night like they do, for some strange reason, one of us would get the others into some kind of trouble. It's like we have a guardian angel that watches over us that gets a kick out of getting one or all of us into some kind of something.

The others didn't answer him, other than shake their heads yes.

They had lots of fun the previous summer; they did seem to get into a lot more trouble than the rest of the kids around town. There had been the little run in with the bull, the fainting goat, and the little trip to the river that didn't do them much good or improve their reputation in Verden.

No, this summer, all five of them made a pact to have fun, lots of fun, but with no trouble involved.

Sonny's mother must have said a thousand times to him last year, "Boy, you have me at my wits' ends; I don't have a clue what to do with you."

"I'll sure enough tell you what to do with that boy." His Grandmother would seem to always chime in. "We could just kill him and his no account friends, go to church Sunday morning and tell God that they just died of something or other."

Sonny knew his grandmother didn't really mean it, because there was always a big old smile on her face whenever she said it.

Sonny knew that his grandmother loved him, would never do anything to harm him, well other than swat him with that stupid old flyswatter she kept with her all day, sleeping with it just in case she got a chance to swat him with it during the night. He caught her with a big smile on her face several times while taking a nap on their old blue couch. He didn't think normal people smiled like she did while sleeping. It even kind of gave him the creeps. He asked her about it one evening. She said she was smiling because in her dreams she got in a couple of good licks on him with the fly swatter.

The boys made plans that morning to meet at the park after class. Some of the classes let out at different times, so whoever got out first would wait for the others to show up.

Sonny and Charlie had Mrs. Eagleton for homeroom. They thought they were pretty darn lucky to get her for homeroom teacher. First, she wasn't very old. They figured around twenty-five. Neither of the boys could build up enough courage to ask her how old she was. That was called "getting too personal," something thirteen year old boys just didn't do.

Bobby Won made that mistake a couple of years ago. The story was still very fresh around the school. Seems Bobby Won had been adopted by a solider from one of the islands the Japanese held during WW11. Bobby's dad moved to Chickasha, a town a few miles from Verden, married a lady that worked at the five and dime, then moved to Verden. Bobby's new step-mom took up with Bobby right from the start, however she changed Bobby's name from Kim Sin Yon to Bobby. Said Kim Sin Yon was way too much of a name for a small boy to have; besides, she said it made her tongued tied trying to say it.

His parents tried to change his last name to their last name, but would have to adopt him in order to do that. There was a problem with that. The solider who found him wandering around wouldn't adopt him until he could take Bobby back to the island where he was found, in order to see if he wanted to live in America or his home island.

The problem was compounded because Bobby's family couldn't afford to take him back for a visit. To add even more to the problem, Bobby's step-dad said that the only way he would ever go back to that godforsaken place would be if someone shot him graveyard dead, and then took his body back. From that day on, Kim Sin Yon was called Bobby Won, no questions asked.

Bobby was four years ahead of Sonny and the boys. What happened when he got too personal with a teacher came to them by word of mouth. We all know how word of mouth sometimes has a way of changing as time goes along or because of the number of times the story is told.

Bobby was in Mrs. Greenwoods' class. Every boy in school tried to get into her class. A couple of the boys that wasn't lucky enough to get in during the year tried to get held back in order to get another shot at it.

Mrs. Greenwoods was very well endowed. "Very well endowed," really weren't the words that most of the boys in Verden used, however. Their words were like "Big Boobs." Some called her, "Giant Tits Greenwoods." Others stuck with, "monster boobs."

There were a lot of the boys, even some of the girls, if they would let it be known, and even some of the other teachers who wondered if they were really all hers, or if part of them might be paper towels or a couple of hand towels rolled up in her bra. One kid thought she might have stuffed her bra with straw, since a person could get it in abundance around the area. Everyone knew better than that because straw would have been sticking out like that scarecrow in the Wizard of Oz. It wouldn't do at all, having a teacher come to school with straw sticking out from under her shirt.

There was more or less of a contest going around school that year. The first person who found out if Mrs. Greenwoods shape was real or not, would win. No one had any idea what they would win, but being the one who found out the truth about the boobs would catapult that person to instant fame, something that would be talked about for years to come. For most that was prize enough.

Every boy in school that was old enough to know what boobs were was after that fame.

Bobby Won wanted to win more than anything else in this world. If he had the chance to get his name changed from Bobby Won to Bobby Simpson or win the boob contest, you can bet he would have chosen boobs hands down. He said "years from now my parents will be dead. Chances are, I will be dead or lying on my death bed somewhere or other and I may not have accomplished anything in life other than finding out about them two boobs. Still, I would have secured my place in history, same as Abraham Lincoln, Custer and even the fellow who discovered America."

One afternoon during math class, Bobby couldn't take it any longer, watching Mrs. Greenwoods sitting at her big brown desk at the head of the class, eating some chips she brought from home that she wasn't able to finish at lunch. When she dropped a couple crumbs on her right breast then brushed them off, that drove Bobby over the edge.

Getting up from his desk, Bobby headed for Mrs. Greenwoods. His eyes were not on the kids he walked by, or on Mrs. Greenwood's eyes. His eyes were on Mrs. Greenwoods' monster boobs. He was a man on a mission.

Reaching her desk, but not looking at her, Bobby said "Crumbs." Nothing else, just "Crumbs." Then, as if he had been doing it all his life, he reached down as if to brush the crumbs off her, but instead he got his finger in between the two buttons holding her shirt together over her monster boobs. With one quick hard jerk, both buttons popped off, one hitting Stacy Zeller just above her right eye. Stacy screamed because she was startled by the flying button. Mrs. Greenwoods screamed when both her bra-covered boobs popped right out of her shirt.

Bobby couldn't say a word. All he could do was look at the two bra-covered boobs that were a few inches from his face. The two boobs filled her complete bra, no rolls of paper towels, no hand towels or any other objects that didn't belong there. There was just boob flesh, boob flesh that was trying to poke out of her bra.

Mrs. Greenwoods jumped up from her chair behind the desk, pulling her shirt together as best she could with her left hand, and with her free right hand, she slapped Bobby with all the might she could muster, knocking him to the floor. You would have thought that slap would have knocked the smile off the boy's face, but if anything, it made him smile even bigger, knowing those crumbs of potato chips and that slap would secure his place in Oklahoma history, if not history throughout the world. Maybe even the people from the island he was born on would raise a statue of him.

Bobby was expelled from school. Mrs. Greenwoods was asked for her resignation because apparently it was against school policy to slap a student with your right hand, even if said student popped your shirt open, exposing your bra and your two monster boobs, thus making you hold your shirt together with your left hand.

Bobby had to move with his folks to Anadarko eight miles away in order to finish school.

Mrs. Greenwoods moved with her husband to a small town in South Dakota.

We heard she and her husband started a sheep farm somewhere not far from the Black Hills.

Chapter Two

After Bruce, Jake, and Gary show up at the park we decided we would go over to Jake's house to hang out until we either decided on something else to do, or we'd go home to supper. It really didn't make that much difference. It was exciting enough just being out of school for the summer.

I planned to spend the night with Bruce that night, something I really didn't care all that much for, but he had been asking me for weeks. I would much rather stay the night with Charlie. His mother always had cake, or homemade candy, something to snack on while watching a few hours of TV.

The only problem with spending the night with Bruce was his seven year old sister Lindsey. Lindsey was a great little girl. She wasn't always under foot like other girls her age, and she stayed mostly to herself if no friends were around to play dolls or make-up with.

The problem was at night. She slept in the same room as Bruce did. Whenever I spent the night, I slept with Bruce in his big double bed. Lindsey slept on her twin bed on the other side of the room. It never failed. Sometime between midnight and first light, she would wake up screaming at the top of her lungs. She would sit straight up in bed and scream.

The first time it happened, I almost wet myself. I was lying there deep asleep, when all of a sudden she started screaming. I had no clue what was going on, seeing her in the dim light sitting up in bed screaming. I was sure a killer had broken in and was about to Murder Lindsey, then Bruce and myself, then on to his parents. I did what any boy my age would do: I started screaming at the top of my lungs as well.

Bruce sat up looking at me as if all of a sudden I went nuts. Lindsey sat there looking at me the way a young girl looks at that old worn out Bear in the Chickasha zoo as if she were see it for the first time.

Bruce started smiling at me. "It's okay. She has nightmares," he said.

"Nightmares!" I answered him, still looking at the little girl who was looking back at me.

"Yes, happens all the time," he said to me as I lay back down.

"By the way, you scream like a little girl," he said snickering.

I made my mind up that would be the last time I would ever spend the night in that house. I like Lindsey a lot, but not enough to sleep in the same room with her. I know that boys my age were not prone to have heart attacks, but one or two more nights of that little girl, my folks would be looking for a spot in the cemetery to put my body.

That's why Bruce had to ask me over and over to spend the night again. Not until he promised that he would get Lindsey to sleep with her parents, did I say I would.

All went well that night. However, I did hear Lindsey scream out early that morning. It didn't scare me this time as much, because as hard as I tried, I just couldn't fall asleep waiting on the little girl to start screaming sometime awful during the night.

After breakfast the next morning, I went home. My grandmother was taking biscuits out of the oven when I got there. "You hungry boy?" she asked.

After just eating toast and gravy at Bruce's house, all I could say was, "Yes." I wasn't really hungry, but my grandmother's biscuits and eggs were to die for. Besides, who was to know if I would be around for lunch. Eat when you get the chance was always my motto.

Charlie came by a few minutes after I finished the last biscuit in the pan. "Boy, you keep eating like that, I might as well call a carpenter over here to widen the doors, because you sure enough won't be able to get through them much longer," s my grandmother said, taking the pan and a couple of plates to the sink.

"Let's go to the depot to talk to Mr. Burger," Charlie said to me.

"Granny is it ok with you if I go to the depot with Charlie?" I asked her.

Before she could answer, Charlie walked up to her, gave her a quick kiss on the cheek and said, "Please Granny. Please."

"Yes! You brats get out of this house before you destroy something," she said smiling at Charlie as she started to pump water into the sink onto the dirty dishes.

"Now if Mr. Burger is busy, you boys leave him alone," s she said to us as we walked out of the kitchen.

We loved talking to the station master, Mr. Burger. He had been everywhere, done just about everything, and we could sit listening to his stories for hours. He had never let us down; he always had a story to tell. I came to the conclusion that his wife probably wouldn't let him talk all that much at home.

If he wasn't hanging the mail for the next train coming, sending or receiving something on the telegraph, then he was always more than glad to tell one or all of us boys one of his stories of life.

We sat on the same the bench used by travelers waiting to catch the train on Wednesdays, the only day the 3:45 stopped here to pick up whoever might be heading to points unknown.

"Boys, have I ever told you about my brother Leroy's first wife?" Mr. Burger asked looking at us from the chair next to the telegraph key.

"Nope," Charlie and I chimed in together, looking at each other.

"Well she was a pistol," he said, kicking back in the chair placing his work boots on the table next to the telegraph key.

"She was a good woman, or at least the two times I met her she seemed mighty fine to me. Always took good care of her husband, my brother Leroy," he said

"She had a problem with itching something awful. When she bought something new, it had to be washed several times before she would even think about putting it on her body. Leroy once told me Angie… his wife's name was Angie. She spent more time naked than wearing anything. Now don't get me wrong. When they was first married, Leroy thought being married to a woman that like, to get naked all the time, was a mighty fine deal. At first, he thought she was doing it for him, but as time went along, he came to realize it was her itching that got her naked. Not his good looks," Mr. Burger said, getting up out of his chair and walking over to the large window that looked out over the tracks.

16

"He took her to about every doctor in Oklahoma City. One gave her some pills, pills that didn't do one little bit of good on that girl's itching. One Doctor gave her a tube of cream to stop the itching. That tube ran out before she was half through putting it on, since every single part of her body itched," he continued.

"Leroy even took her to a woman over to Clinton that was into voodoo. She put some of Angie's hair in a big old wooden pot with a couple of chicken feathers, a few bones, a couple of duck eggs that she said was from a one legged duck, and a picture of Abe Lincoln. If you wonder why the picture of Lincoln, it was to get the itching demon to take up residence in Mr. Lincoln's body, wherever that body may be," he said to us as he sat down next to Charlie on the old bench.

"Anyways, this old woman did some chanting over the bowl, some dancing around the room. Every once in a while, she would beat the continents in the bowl using a can of creamed corn, since someone stole the wooden spoon she normally used. Well, all that dancing around and beating the eggs did absolutely no good on the itching. The only relief anyone got out of all that dancing was the twenty- two dollars the old lady relieved Leroy of," he said, turning and grinning at us.

I hoped he didn't mind my and Charlie's smiles, but I couldn't help but picture some old woman dancing around a room with a can of creamed corn, beating a bunch of junk in a bowl. I was sure that picture in my mind would stay with me for the rest of my life.

"Leroy did more than I believe any other man would have done for his wife. He bought creams out the yin yang, had a closet plum full of creams from bottom to top, and spent all his money on Doctors from here to yonder, trying to get that confounded itching to stop. I sure enough am glad to tell you this: if it was my Mrs. Burger, I'm sure I would have given up long before Leroy did. Heck boys, he didn't even have extra cash for things he needed, much less for things he wanted," Mr. Burger said, moving back to the chair by the telegraph key.

"How it all ended, Leroy came home from work one evening to find Angie gone. In their bedroom, lying square on her pillow, was a note written on a piece of an old white flour bag, "GONE TO ICELAND, AIN'T COMING BACK, Angie."

Mr. Burger turned his attention to the sound coming from the telegraph key. Deciding it wasn't for him, he went back to his story.

"That young girl just up and moved to Iceland. Someone, somewhere, told her that the air in Iceland was as pure as them nun's living over to the convent in Chickasha. All Leroy could do was file for a divorce, try to live a normal life without his itching wife a scratching and complaining, scratching and complaining every minute she was awake. And that was a lot, since she couldn't sleep much, her body itching like it did. Anyways, I'm sure Leroy is better off, and for Angie, she is more likely than not married to some fellow in Iceland that makes his living catching fish," he said, scratching the back of his head and looking down at the papers lying all around on his desk.

When the key started clicking again, Mr. Burger grabbed a pen to write down the incoming message.

We knew that story time was over when he did that.

Charlie and I decided to walk over to Bruce's house to see what he was up to. When we got there, Bruce and Gary were sitting on the porch talking with a couple of suitcases sitting beside them.

"You going somewhere?" Charlie asked

"My dad got a job on the ranch way down by Hugo. It's only for a couple of weeks, so he is going to let me and Gary go with him. He said three could stay in the motel for the same price as one, so I asked Gary to come and keep me company," he said, looking first to me then Charlie.

"Well the room may be the same price for three as one, but when he has to bail you guys out of jail, you can bet it will cost a lot more." Charlie said, smiling at me.

"Jail, what are you talking about jail?" Bruce asked anyone that would answer.

"Hugo is Choctaw country. There are more Choctaw Indians in that area then anywhere in the world. I've been told if you throw a rock hard, and I mean *hard*, you can knock down three of them every time you chunk the rock. So, if you aren't part Indian of some kind or other, they will put you smooth into jail just for being on Indian land," I said to them.

"Tell you what you might do, you can go over to my house, gather up a bunch of chicken feathers, then when you're milling around Hugo, let them chicken feathers hang out from all your pockets. It's a bad omen for a Choctaw to touch man or woman with feathers hanging out of their pockets," I said, trying not to smile.

"That is pure bull crap," Gary answered, trying to smile.

"Nope. Just as true as true can be. You guys know I am part Choctaw on my father's side of the family. Heck, I'm 1/32 Choctaw, so if anyone in town was to know about Choctaw rituals, that person would be me," I said, with a straight face this time.

19

I was telling them the truth, well the truth about my Choctaw blood. All the other was just pure bull, but Charlie and I sure couldn't let them leave for two weeks without trying to jerk them around some That would have been pure un-American on our part.

I kind of hated teasing them about the Choctaws. However, it was true Hugo was Choctaw country. The part that wasn't true was that the Choctaws were mean. The Choctaws are about the friendliest people around. They will go out of their way to help one another, or anyone else for that matter.

We said our goodbyes to them. I headed home, and Charlie did the same.

Chapter Three

When I got home, my grandmother was in an uproar about Stella Fulbright. Apparently she looked at my granny at the bank. Stella was a woman about the same age as Granny. 'Course no one knew my grandmother's age, or at least not anyone that would tell me. When I asked her how old she was, she always had the same thing to say, "Boy, you're as old as you feel, and I feel twenty-five, so I guess that makes me twenty-five."

I made the mistake of answering back once "The chances of you being twenty-five are about the same chance Custer had to win that battle at the Bighorn."

She happened to have the flyswatter with her. Before I could get away, she connected three good licks across my back.

"Come back here, boy, and I'll whip the hide plum off you," s she answered, trying to hide her laughter.

I asked my mother, once, why Granny seemed to get her panties in a wad when Stella Fulbright's name was brought up.

She told me that when she was a little girl, seven or eight years old, Granny and Stella were good friends. They did their canning together. Many a time, when one of their family members came down with something, the other would be right there to help out. They lived about a mile apart. Granny had an old mule she called Speedy. Granny either hitched Speedy to their old wagon, or if she figured no one would see, she road bareback to see Stella. Riding bareback in those days was something a young woman just didn't do. It was not ladylike. Two things that were pure no-no's back then were for a woman to show her legs or ride a horse or mule anyway other than sidesaddle.

There was a girl back then that became the town harlot just because she rode an old horse to town bareback. I was told her name was Kay Heck. People said she was a nice girl, but when she showed up on that horse with her leg exposed to a few inches above the knee, that was all the town needed to get rumors started about Kay.

One rumor had her working in a house of ill repute on Choctaw avenue in Chickasha People said she was working as the bartender, serving drinks to the old men that came in to watch the girls dance. Rumor had it, she would double up on the alcohol she put in the men's drink. When they got drunk enough and fell off the bar stool, she took the money out of their wallets.

One afternoon, Little Pa, Stella's oldest boy, showed up really excited about a problem his father was having. He said his dad had eaten something Stella left for him while she and the other children went to Verden to pick up the supplies to carry them through the month.

Being the friend Granny was, she hitched old Speedy to the wagon went straight over to see if she could help the old man in any way.

People said when Granny got there it was the most awful sight she had ever encountered in all her life. She said she had seen a fellow get hit by a train once, seen a friends milk cow hit by lighting a couple of minutes after it happened, seen several babies being cut out of their mothers cause they was way too big to be born the natural way. This sight was worse than any of those.

Opening the Fulbright's front door and seeing Pa Fulbright leaning over the kitchen sink trying to toss up everything he had eaten the last few days was bad enough, but seeing the condition his body was in was another story. He had lost control of his bowls. It was all over him. Every place he walked or stood there was a puddle. It seemed to be everywhere. Granny wondered how Pa could still be alive, much less still standing after all this.

Granny tried to talk to him, but in his weakened state, Pa Fulbright made no sense. Granny cleaned him up best as she could, worked for hours getting everything else cleaned. Getting the smell out of the house was the worst of all. It was a lucky thing people were cooking on wood stoves back then, because she found some green hickory she burnt in the wood stove, as well as in the fireplace. It took several pieces of hickory a couple of hours of burning to get the bad smell out and the hickory smell in.

Granny was still worried about Pa the way he was acting. He was talking out of his head. She realized it had to be a virus, not something he had eaten at all. There was no doctor anywhere close at the time, so all she could do was give him some homemade colloidal silver, something her mother showed her how to make when she was a teen.

Granny was on her way back to the house from the outside facility when Stella and the kids pulled up in the wagon. Stella jumped off the wagon in confusion when she saw Granny standing on the front porch. They walked in the front door together. Standing right there in front of the two women was Pa, just as naked as the day he first arrived on this Earth.

Since Pa was still in his confusion, he walked, more like stumbled, to Granny, grabbed her like a long lost friend, and planted a big kiss square on her lips. Before she could push him away, he turned, said hi to his wife, stumbled over to a chair by the window, fell into it and then passed out as soon as his naked butt hit the seat.

"What in God's name have you and Pa been doing, you hussy," Stella said to my Grandmother.

"What... what did you say"? Granny asked.

"I work my tail off taking care of this family. What do I get in return? My so-called friend and my no-account, no-good for nothing husband playing footsies soon as my back is turned!," Stella obviously didn't know that Pa had passed out without hearing a word, or knowing what anger he had caused, both Stella's and the anger that Stella's words had just stirred up in Granny.

My grandmother was always kind of slow to anger, but this was apparently all it took this time. I was told she didn't say a word to Stella. Instead, she walked out to the outhouse, picked up the bucket she used to clean the floors. That bucket contained all the yuck and the old rags she had used to make the outhouse smell as good as all outdoors. Granny carried it back to the front door. When she saw Stella standing in the middle of the room, all high and mighty, Granny called up all the might she could muster and let the contents of that bucket fly across the room, hitting Stella just above where her belly button was under her dress.

Stella said, "What the heck!" Before she could get another word, out the smell struck her. She ran for the front door, getting sick along the way.

"I wouldn't have that man if he was the last man on earth, had hundred dollar bills popping out of his butt every five seconds, or if you offered him to me on a silver platter. Granny said to Stella as my grandmother got in her wagon and gave Speedy a hard rap with the back of the rains.

After she found out the real reason that Granny was with her husband, Stella came by a couple of times to apologize to Granny. The first time that Stella showed up, my grandmother shot at her with her old 12 gage shotgun before Stella could get within a 100 yards of Granny's place.

Another time when they met in front of the bank, Stella said something to Granny.

"Bitch don't talk to me, don't come around me again, don't talk to anyone in my family, for that matter don't even try to talk to my dogs when you go by the road in front of my house, cause if you do, I will find you, beat you with in an inch of your life, then when you heal up from that beating, I'll look you up and beat your no good blaming ass again,," s Granny had told Stella before turning and walking away.

From that day on, Stella and my grandmother stopped talking. It was, more or less, an un-written rule that when Stella went to town on Wednesdays and Fridays, Granny would stay home. All the other days, when town was Stella-free, my grandmother would go if she wanted to get something in town.

To this day, if my grandmother happens to find out I played with, or was friends with any of Stella's family, I would have heck to pay. I'm not sure, but I bet she would have pulled me out of school altogether. My grandmother would rather me be an uneducated fool than associate with anyone in Stella's family.

Chapter Four

Charlie, Jake and I decided one morning we would go down to the river bridge, make a raft out of whatever we could find and then float a couple of miles down the river, just like that explorer Cortez fellow did back in the olden days, like our history teacher was always trying to drive into our head.

Charlie brought an ax and some rope. I brought some rope myself and a hack saw. Jake brought some boloney, a loaf of bread and a mason jar full of water.

We found some old trees that had either died because they got struck by lightning or bugs killed them. These tress had long fallen over, or was blown over by a tornado or one of the strong winds that seem to come around almost every March.

We tied what we could of those together. Charlie chopped a few smaller trees down to make the raft a little bigger and I tried to help with the hack saw, which was no use at all. Come to find out, a hack saw is only used on metal. It isn't worth a plug nickel cutting down small trees.

When we boys decided the raft was river-worthy, the three of us pushed it into the water. Once we were on, we used the poles we cut to push ourselves into the slow moving current. We sat down and started making ourselves boloney sandwiches. For some reason, everything seemed to go well for a change. No one dropped anything in the water, or fell in.

We slowly floated along several minutes talking, telling jokes and telling one another what our plans were for the future.

Jake hoped to get into college. He loved football. He went every time he got a chance to go see one of the high school games in Chickasha, or Anadarko. In fact, he jumped at the chance to go. He said he would like to go to Oklahoma University to try to play football there. The only holdup would be he had never set foot on a football field, which might be a small problem his first day or two of practice.

I tried to explain to him that he had a better chance getting a job pulling the heads off pigeons than playing football in college.

"I've never heard of any jobs pulling pigeon heads off," he answered.

"Well, I haven't heard of all that many football players that don't know how to play either," I said back to him.

Charlie said he wanted to be a movie star, working with Jimmy Stewart, and the love of his life was Kim Novak.

All of us boys went to see Vertigo one Saturday afternoon. After the movie let out, Charlie informed us right in front of the theater that he was going to leave Verden the same day he graduated from high school, not the next day, but on the very day he graduated. Said he would pack his bags the night before graduation. He would walk off the stage, and then he would keep walking all the way to the nearest bus station and catch the first bus going to Hollywood. When he got to Hollywood, he would get a hold of one of them fellows selling maps of the stars homes he heard about from his uncle Dale.

When he had the map, he would buy a couple of roses if they weren't too expensive. If they were too expensive, he would only pick up one. He might add a candy bar in place of the second rose. Then he head straight for Miss Novak's house and knock on her door. When Kim answered, he would explain right then and there, that he was in pure love with her and that if she didn't have a big problem with it, he would like to marry her and move right in.

"Right! You better start smoking before you do all that," I told him.

"Start smoking? Why smoking?" he asked.

"Well, just as soon as you knock on that door, tell her all that bull crap, the cops are going to lock you up for years, lot of years. At least if you smoked, you would have something to do with all that extra time on your hands," I said, laughing at him.

"Make jokes about it, but you don't have a clue what it's like to be in love, real love, pure honest love," he said to me while looking at Jake.

"What're you going to do if her husband opens the door, not her?"

Well, if she is married and her husband opens the door, I will do what any normal guy in love with another man's wife does," he said turning to me.

"And what is that?" I asked

"Turn, run like heck and hope I can get out of sight before he can find his revolver," he answered, turning around with a big old grin on his face.

We floated for what seemed like a couple of hours. None of us had a watch. They were too expensive. If any of us had a watch, we wouldn't have brought it on a float trip and take a chance of losing it in the muddy river water.

Floating halfway around a sharp bend, we heard people talking. Not knowing who it might be, we thought it would be kind of a smart thing to head over to the river bank, do some investigating. You never know who might be talking. There was a good chance it was a couple of people doing a little fishing, however on the other hand, fifty some years ago a young girl was killed on this very river, so it paid to not take chances. Who's to know it could very well be gangsters that just robbed a bank in Oklahoma City, or someplace even closer, hiding on the river bank until the heat was off. Just as soon as we floated into their sight they might pull their rods or machine guns, and kill all three of us, just as dead as dead could be. We boys had seen plain enough what a Tommy Gun could do to a body in all the James Cagney movies we went to on Saturday afternoons.

Pushing our raft toward the shore, I made a motion to the others to be quiet, or at the very least to whisper if they just had to say something.

When I stepped onto the banks edge, I whispered that I would go look and for them to wait there for me. I might as well been talking to that old tree branch floating by, because they both started shaking their heads, no.

"You may need help," Jake whispered.

Help my foot. They were just afraid to stay there, or on the other hand they didn't want to be left out if I stumbled onto someone like Al Capone. They wanted to be in on it as well, and so they could go back to town and brag to everyone just like I had plans to do.

Duck walking, crawling, moving bent over, we moved through the trees and the underbrush toward the voices we heard.

When we were, what we thought, right up on them, we parted a bunch of Johnson grass. There in front of us was none other than Curtis Elbert and Kelly Woodson sitting on a blanket. Kelly was a senior, and Curtis graduated last year.

"Good gosh Kelly we been dating for God knows how long. Don't you think it's about time I got to a base other than first base." Curtis seemed to be begging Kelly.

"Nope! You know nothing like that is just about to happen until I have a big old diamond right here on my finger,," s she said to him pointing at the finger on her left hand.

"You better be happy with what you have now,," s she said

"You know I am. I love you Kelly. It's just so hard to wait, and you have no idea what it's like for a man. A friend of mine was telling me about a guy in about the same boat as I am right here and now. This guy said his girlfriend wouldn't let him do anything more than what you let me do. Said it caused him to have a stroke. Said he is no more than a vegetable now days. Lays in his mother's fruit cellar on a cot. He doesn't have a clue where he is. He could be lying in the Taj Mahal for all he knows. Said his ma can only feed him soft food like mashed potatoes, gravy, and such. That poor boy will never know what it's like to bite into a good old steak again. Never be able to go to the movie, or kiss his girl again,," he said to Kelly in the same begging tone.

"I'm not about to believe any of that. You're only saying that to get what you want,," s she answered

"Well it's a pure fact. I don't think anyone keep any statistic on the such, but it wouldn't surprise me one little bit it there isn't young men lying in fruit cellars all over the world, just because their girlfriends are so blasted pure," he said this not so much begging, but as a matter of fact.

Kelly lay back on the blue blanket, placing her head on a large pillow the couple brought with them.

This was more than we could have ever asked for. If we had lost all the food in the water, or had gotten wet getting on the raft, spying on this couple would have made it all better. All we could do was wink at one another and do our best not to laugh out loud.

As Curtis was lying beside the young girl named Kelly, he started kissing her. First little kisses, then they became longer and longer. He moved his hand under her blue blouse just a little. Before he could move it anymore, she grabbed his hand and moved it away from her stomach. This happened several more times.

We soon became bored watching them when something different happened. This time, when he tried to move his hand under her blouse, she didn't stop him. Curtis was obviously feeling good with what he was getting away with, so he started to unbutton her blouse. Charlie and Jake looked at me at the same time smiling. We knew what all those prospectors felt like when they finely found that vein of gold, what all the men felt like when they found out WW11 was over. We were about to see something we were sure no other thirteen year old boys had ever seen before in America.

There it was, the last button. Kelly lay with her blouse wide open for Curtis, God, and we three boys to see.

I couldn't help myself. It was something I had to do, and it might be the way I was raised. I stood up out of the couple's sight and shouted at the top of my lungs. "Over here Dad. I think we can get to river over here."

Lying back down Jake and Charlie looked at me like I had just lost my mind, that in less than a second I had gone from a normal thirteen year old boy, to a complete, raving maniac.

You would have thought someone poured hot water all over the couple. Kelly sat up trying to button her blouse. At the same time she also tried to stand. Curtis seemed to be trying to button it as well, however he was so startled and so upset hearing me holler out, that he was unbuttoning her blouse. She would get one buttoned; he would unbutton it. I have no idea how long this would have went on until she hit his hand and screamed, "STOP!"

When she finely got all the buttons together, she stood next to his car while he picked up the blanket and pillow. That put away, they stood there just as if they were in the foyer of the First Baptist Church.

We never did know what they ended up doing. We snuck out of there before our laughing gave us away. We made a pact never to let anyone know what we did, even Bruce and Gary when they got back. It would be just like those two to tell Curtis it was us that ruined his fun. There was a very good chance Curtis wouldn't just beat us up. There was a chance he might just kill all three of us for doing what we just did. Now, because of us, one day he will be laying in his folk's fruit cellar.

Chapter Five

The next morning Charlie and I met Jake at his house. His uncle Dan was coming in from Dallas. Dan got a weekend pass from the Veterans Hospital. I felt sorry for him thinking he was wounded fighting either the Japanese or Germans in the war. Come to find out he got drunk and fell off the curb in front of a empty milk truck somewhere in California. Never did see any action, other than the milk truck's wheel rolling over his pelvis. He had been in the hospital a little over a year and then in a full body cast for six months. This was his first ten-day pass since the accident.

Jake tried to explain his uncle was a bit strange. He wasn't sure how he got to be so strange. Jake thought his Uncle Dan's mother might have dropped him on his head when he was a baby. No one in the family had any idea how he got the way he was. Some seemed to think he might have gotten into some rat poison, or he could even have contracted a virus of some kind that went straight to his brain.

My grandmother met Dan once in Rush Springs, on Watermelon day they have each year. When she came home, she stated, in no uncertain terms, that he was a nut, simple as that. A nut that they should send to Norman, that mental place, and get him a card stating that he was a nut. That way he would be a card-carrying nut then, when he went and done something only a nut could think of, he could pull out the card, showing whoever, that he was a nut. That way, he was more than likely not going to get into as much trouble as a nut with no card.

His uncle Dan was afraid of just about everything, tornados, earthquakes, Indians, Mexicans, well Mexicans if they happen to be wearing a sombrero. Men and women from China was a complete different matter. He would turn around take off in a dead run if he happen to see a Chinese person walking his way.

He was deathly afraid of anything that might in anyway hurt him, guns, knives. He wouldn't even play baseball as a kid because of the way a bat looked.

When he was drafted into the Unites States Army, he made it halfway thorough boot camp. When he was sent to the practice grenade range, he passed out when they handed him a grenade to throw.

He spent three weeks in the hospital. When he received his first weekend pass for good behavior, he was run over by a milk wagon.

The Army has the idea he jumped in front of the milk wagon because of his fear of everything that he had o face in boot camp. He was very lucky he only broke his pelvis in four places instead of killing himself when that wagon wheel was running over his pelvis. I bet he would have been happy to toss that grenade or shoot his weapon at the shooting range when he felt the pain of that wagon wheel.

When Jake's uncle finely got there, he was in no shape to meet anyone. Apparently he must have got hold of some sipping whiskey on his way home and sipped it until he didn't have a clue who he was anymore.

Jake helped his mother put his uncle to bed. I didn't want any part of that, so I waited outside by the old tire swing in the back yard, if you wanted to call it a back yard. If someone was to walk up on the yard without knowing the family living here, they might think it was the start of a pretty good junk yard.

There was an old fifty-five gallon barrel someone had cut the top out of to make a homemade barbeque pit. Looked like the last time it was used, or cleaned for that matter, had to be long before I was born. In one corner, there were two old hot water tanks that someone used for target practice. Across the yard from that was three and a half rolls of old rusty chicken wire someone must have taken down tried to roll up, doing a pretty lousy job. Next to the wire sat an old bath tub. Apparently the same person that shot up the hot water tanks had a few extra bullets and had used them on the tub.

When Jake came back outside he was carrying what looked like a Prince Albert cigar box. He looked as if he had just run face to face into a ghost. His face was as white as the sheets on my bed. His hands were shaking something awful; when he got up close to me, I could hear something rattling around in the cigar box that sounded like a large rock.

"What the heck is wrong with you?" I asked, trying to smile, not knowing if I should be smiling the way he looked.

"Uncle Dan handed me this box then told me to go fishing,," he answered.

I understood then what was in the box: fishing tackle. That was the reason it sounded like rocks, I thought.

"Tackle?" I asked

Sitting down and placing his back against the tree to help support himself, he said, "I guess you could call it fishing tackle," he handed the box up to me.

I took it and smiled down at him, opening the cigar box. If there had been a mirror around, I'm sure my face would have been as white as Jake's. In fact, the way I felt looking in the box, mine could have even been whiter because the blood had drained out of it. As I looked into the box, I felt my knees getting weak. They both felt like they were going to buckle on me.

In that cigar box was a real, honest to goodness pineapple, or what they called a grenade in all the war movies we boys had ever seen. I wanted to drop it, but for some reason, I couldn't wait to get away from the thing. All I knew about grenades was what I saw John Wayne, Gary Cooper and a few other actors do in the movies.

I fell down next to Jake and handed the box back to him. The only words I knew to say were, "Damn it, boy."

Jake didn't answer me. He just took the box and leaned his head back against the tree trunk.

"Well?" I asked

"Hold your water. I'm thinking." he answered me.

We both sat there for several minutes just leaning against the tree. I'm not sure how long, but I know it was long enough to make my head start to hurt. I wasn't sure if it was hurting from leaning against the tree, or from being so nervous sitting this close to an object that, if went off, anyone looking for us would only be able to find our PF Flyer tennis shoes.

"Let's do what Uncle Dan said," Jake finely said.

"And what might that be? Pray tell."

"Fishing. Let's go fishing," h

"Think we may run into someone we might have to use a grenade on?" I asked, pushing the lid down on the cigar box that Jake was holding open. I didn't care to look at the thing.

"No, stupid. This is the bait,," he answered. The color was coming back in his face, along with a smile.

"Bait," I answered.

Jake didn't answer me with words. Instead he made motions with his hands, acting as if he had an imaginary grenade in his hand. He stuck it into his mouth, the same way actors did in the movies. Then, he made like he had the pin in his mouth, pulling the pin with his teeth. Finally, he made the motion of throwing it into the river.

"I'll go get Charlie." I said. "We'll meet you in the park. For God's sake don't be stupid with that thing, well anymore stupider than you normally are." I said, smiling as I turned to leave.

"We'll meet you at the Washita River Bridge," I hollered out over my shoulder.

I told Charlie about the grenade on the way to the bridge. He thought I was lying. Said he had lots of uncles and not a single one of them ever brought him a grenade. I tried to explain to him that this was a once in a lifetime opportunity. If Jake didn't have a half crazy uncle, a uncle who was in the Army, a uncle that spent most of his wakening hours drinking or hunting something to drink, we wouldn't be making this trip to the bridge.

When we boys met on the bridge, we couldn't decide whether to go down to the water's edge and toss it in from there. If we went to the water's edge, we would be close enough to jump in, if we needed to throw back what fish we blew up.

Charlie had a better idea. He thought it would be a lot better if we just threw it off the bridge. That way we stood a lot better chance that one, or all of us, would not lose an arm or leg, or even getting killed.

We boys made a pact, standing on the bridge, that if one of us were to get killed, the other one or ones left alive would talk the dead guy's folks in not sending the body to the local funeral pallor. We had a situation last summer with the funeral home, and what we thought was a real live zombie, turned out to be a drowning victim, not a zombie at all it did, however, turn us completely off the Verden funeral home.

"Well here goes," Jake said.

He placed the little ring that held the safety pin in place between his teeth, then he gave the grenade a hard jerk just like he was John Wayne himself, only when John Wayne did it one of his top two teeth didn't chip off.

We had to end up using my buck knife and a rock to bend the two little prongs that kept the pin from being pulled out by accident closer together, and then it took Jake to hold onto the thing with both hands, while Charlie pulled the pin.

Once the pin was out Jake kept a firm grip on the handle. He knew enough that as long as you held onto the handle it wouldn't go off. We weren't real sure just how long a person had once you let it go.

I moved a few feet away from Jake, toward the north end of the bridge. Charlie went south.

Jake leaned over the edge of the bridge and let it go.

Charlie peered over the railing not moving from right where he was just at. I did the same thing.

The thing hit the water just like any old rock we ever tossed in, but this time, before the splash it made could settle down, there was a woof sound, then a blast that had to wake anyone sleeping with in a quarter mile of the place The bridge had to be at least a hundred feet above the water, however the spray still hit us boys.

When our sense of hearing came back to somewhat normal, we heard screaming down below the bridge. All we could think of was that we must have killed someone, or at least hurt them real, real bad.

We couldn't think of anything other to do but run, taking off toward town. We stopped when the screaming turned to laughter.

Peeking through the tall weeds, we saw the Reverend Emmitt McGraw, his wife, Judy, their boy, Alta, and their young daughter, Mary Ben. The kids were laughing jumping up and down. Reverend Emmitt was in the water up to his waist throwing fish up to his wife, Judy, on the bank.

He would grab a big old Catfish, toss it up to his wife, raise his hands and holler at the top of his lungs, "Praise the Lord. Praise the Lord!"

His wife on the bank would sing out after each praise that came from her husband, "That's right. That's right. That's what we're talking about, Lord. That's right."

Seeing we hadn't mangled or killed anyone, we parted the weeds and went down where the family was praising,

"Hi, Mr. McGraw. You okay?" I asked.

"Boys, are we ever glad to see you. See all these fish?" he asked, pointing at the fish floating around him.

We shook our heads yes.

"Well boys, if you had been here no more than one minute ago, you three would have seen, no, you would have witnessed a true, I'm talking a true, ever-loving, card carrying miracle, and something just as big as big can be," h

His wife chimed in with "That's right. You tell them, honey, and you tell these boys, make them believe. Make these boys believers, just like you and me. Yes, believers!"

The kids were still dancing around. I'm not sure they were interested so much in a miracle as they were in dancing around.

"Boys, no more than a couple of minutes ago, this whole family was wadded up right here in prayer. I'm sure you haven't heard, but we are going to have a fish fry at our church. You boys know I'm the preacher over to the Christian Church don't you?" he asked.

"Yes, sir," Jake answered him.

I said, "We've sure been meaning to come one of these Sundays." I have no idea why I said it. There wasn't a bit of truth in it. If it wasn't for our folks, we wouldn't even go to our own church, much less volunteer to go to some other church on our own.

The preacher just looked at me with a yes, yes I'm sure you have, look.

"Like I was saying, we were in family prayer, praying for the Lord to grant us a good day of fishing, the ability to catch enough fish to feed all thirty-two of our congregation this Sunday evening. With our eyes closed in prayer, there was a sudden explosion, water going every which of way. Fish started to rise to the surface. Hearing and seeing this, we knew one of the Lords angels had struck the water with the power that only one can muster up by being an angel," h

"I tell you boys, it was a site to behold. I only wished I had been looking at the water when it all happened. Lord I would love to have seen that winged messenger of our Lord and

Savior. That angel had to be riding a great horse when he struck the water with the mighty staff angels are known to carry," he said

"I thought angles had wings Daddy," The little girl said.

"Sure they do, honey. Some have wings. Some ride mighty steeds,," he answered her

"Why… why don't all angles have wings?" she continued

"Well, I recon that's determined by what degree of an angel you are. The big powerful angels all have wings like Gabriel, but angles that haven't done a lot in Heaven haven't gotten wings yet,," he answered her.

"Done a lot. Done a lot of what?" she asked.

"You could tell he was getting kind of irritated at her when he said, "Well, angels start out as just your run of the mill guardian angel, keeping people from getting hit by trains, from drowning, getting them out of houses when a fire starts and such, then, when they have saved whatever number it is that they have to save, the archangel Gabriel goes up and tells that new angel that he will be getting a might steed. I figure after he does things like we just saw here a few times for people, then he gets his wings," he told her.

That seemed to satisfy the girl, so he turned his attention back to us.

If they only knew the truth: while their eyes were closed in prayer, we three boys from the top of that old bridge came within an inch of their lives to making angels out of all four of them.

We kept what happened that day just between the three of us. We were worried that if the truth were to get out, there was a chance we might end up in juvenile detention center in Chickasha.

It did, however, make great conversation for the people of town about the day the angel struck the Washita River, bringing forth fish for the multitude of the Christian Church. There was even a few of the church people that wanted to put up some sort of a statue of an angel striking the water with a staff. Thank goodness, they gave up that idea. It is a very well-known fishing spot however to this day.

Chapter Six

A couple of days after the grenade fiasco, we three boys decided we would just take it easy, sit around our little park and watch the world go by.

There is no way three thirteen year old boys can just let the world go by without getting involved in something. This something was a haunted house that Mr. Knapp had told us about.

Mr. Knapp just happened to be sitting in the park that day smoking. His wife Shirley was a down home Baptist that didn't believe in dancing, smoking, cussing, or anything else other than praying. Shirley was against just about everything, so Mr. Knapp had to come to the park to smoke his cigarettes. He only lived about a half block from the park, so he didn't care all that much. Said it got him away from Shirley. Said he planned to stop smoking, but he figured something out. It took him fifteen minutes to come to the park and smoke this he did three times a day, which added up to forty five minutes a day. That added up to a little over five hours a week, or a bit over two hundred fifty hours a year, or around twenty days. Add that to the time he is sleeping, and between the smoking and the sleeping, he is away from his Bible packing wife a heck of a lot. Said if smokes didn't cost so much he would become a chain smoker. Then the only time he would have to be around his wife would be when he was eating, or in bed, and when they were in bed, they were both sleeping so that didn't even count.

As he smoked, he started telling us the story of Wanda Bagwell, who once lived about a mile and a half east of town.

Wanda had been married to Bryant only three days when Bryant got himself caught up in his hay bailer. Before he could get away from the thing, it pulled him in along with the alfalfa he was bailing.

Wanda had lunch fixed for him. When he didn't show up, she went looking for him. She found his tractor and bailing machine going in circles in the field, but couldn't find her husband anywhere. Everyone in town came out to help look for Bryant. They looked for hours that day, and for a few days more until they gave up the search.

There was lots of speculation about what might have happen to Bryant. Some thought he didn't care for married life at all. They thought that he just picked up, hitchhiked to Anadarko and caught the Greyhound to points unknown.

There were a few people who thought that Wanda did away with him to collect the insurance money. That theory was soon put to rest when it was found that there was only insurance on the four cows they owned, none on Wanda, or Bryant.

Mr. Duckworth, with his two hired hands, came over to help Wanda load the bales of hay and get them into the barn.

When the truck was about half loaded, the boy throwing the bails up let out a curdling scream and dropped the bail he was holding. Wanda thought she must have rolled the truck over his foot. She jumped out of the truck to see if she could help him. She also let out a scream when she saw her husband's face entangled in the bale of hay.

They found different body parts in several bales throughout the field.

From that day on ,Wanda was never the same. She stopped talking to people when she came to town to pick up her mail or get groceries. It wasn't long until she stopped coming to town altogether. If she needed something she would just have it delivered. When the delivery boy got to her house with the food, he would find the money in a small blue bowl a rock placed on top of the money. If it was windy that day, the money would be in the bowl sitting on a chair next to the door. The delivery boy would place Wanda's things there, take the money and leave, never seeing Wanda.

In time, her calls to the store stopped. Some of the town's people became concerned and sent the Sheriff to check on her. He found Wanda, actually, it was Wanda's body, hanging in the living room, suspended from the ceiling fan.

Since Wanda didn't have any relatives, the bank took the place over. Since the bank could not find any buyers for the place because of the morbid history, the place fell into disrepair.

For some time, kids would park out there to party, drink their beer, do some necking, until strange stories started to come from the kids. Some said they saw Wanda looking out the second story window, while others said they saw Bryant walking around in the field next to the house. He looked like he was hunting something. The kids figured, more than likely, he was looking for the parts of his body that the bailer chopped up.

That was enough for the three of us. We decided right then and there we would check the place out first thing in the morning. We could have gone out there this day, however it was getting a bit late and we wouldn't want to get out there and then get caught in the place after dark.

We made all kinds of excuses to one another why we should wait until tomorrow, but the truth was when you're thirteen years old, hearing a story like the one we just heard brought the coward out of all three of us. Not one of us would ever admit we were afraid of anything. In reality, this little story did the trick, because we would go out there alright, but when we went the sun would be in the sky.

We left the next morning around eight A.M. from my house. Charlie came up with an old machete that had seen much better days. The blade was completely covered with rust. It looked like someone used it as a hammer more often than need be, and it was all hacked up with dents all along the cutting edge.

"Where did you get that piece of crap?" I asked him.

"You just never mind where I got it. You will be darn glad I have this if we happen to run into Bryant or Wanda,," he answered me.

"Your folks buy you books and buy you books, and all you ever do is eat the backs off them. You know just as well as I do that you can't kill a ghost with no rusty old machete." I said, laughing at him.

"You need to read those books not just chew on the backs. Ghosts are dead. That's the main requirement to become a ghost," I said to him as we walked along.

"Well it makes me feel safe,," he said

"That's about the only thing it will do," I answered

48

Walking along dirt road, we came across a pasture with several cows. One was the biggest brown bulls I have ever seen. I couldn't help myself when I asked Charlie, "Say, Charlie, would you like to try a little Bull nut slapping again. There is your target standing right over there, and for Christ sakes, look at the nuts on that bull," I said, laughing out loud.

"I can see you would like me to use this machete on you,," he answered with a sour look on his face.

"Sure didn't take long for Charlie to get tired of that game did it?" Jake chimed in laughing

"Nope, he might not be the smartest melon in the patch, however he figured out bull nut slapping is not for him," I said

We made a slight right turn around a large growth of sunflower plants. Soon as we turned, we saw it, a large white two story house. From the distance, it looked like a mansion to us boys, but most two story homes did look like mansions to us, since we all came from such meager backgrounds.

As we got a little closer, the place took on a more sinister look. Most of the white paint was peeling off the front of the house. You could see that the two large white pillars that were holding up the awning over the front porch were cracked and weather worn from lack of any attention at all over the years.

Just walking up to the house gave us the creeps. If this had been any other house around for a hundred miles that looked like this one, we would just have thought it was old, and in need of some work.

The story that went along with this place is what gave us the creeps. It wasn't the house at all but the two ghosts that stayed here that creeped us out so much.

Standing in front of the place, I secretly wished I had also brought me a machete, even if it too was worn out like Charlie's.

"Well there she is," Jake said

"Yep there she is," I answered.

"Crap, look!" Jake said pointing at one of the upstairs windows.

Looking up we saw an old dingy white Curtin flapping out of the window in the warm summer breeze.

"Wind," I said to no one in particular.

It's strange how little we boys talked to one another when we were stressed out. We spoke in the shortest sentences we could come up with. If we could get our point across with one single word, well that was all the better. It was as if talking around a haunted house would wake up whatever it was that haunted the place. The less you talk, the better chance it was that you would be left alone.

"Should we go in?" I asked.

"It would sure enough be ashamed to come all the way out here to just turn around and leave," Charlie said, looking first at me and then at Jake.

"But if you guys would rather leave, I believe in majority rules," Charlie said.

"Well, let's at least go in past the front door. That way, if someone were to ask, we could tell them we went in. Don't think it would be all that necessary to tell them just how far we went into the place," he said.

"Okay then, let's do this," I answered back.

"We three stepped up on the large porch at the same time. Charlie turned the front door knob, giving the door a little push as he did. The squeaking sound sounded loud enough to be heard in downtown Verden. It's strange how a little squeak gets modified so much when it is connected to something haunted.

Stepping into what looked like once was a very fine large living room, we boys just stood there looking around, moving only our heads.

As we started to move just a little, our eyes started to became accustom to our surroundings. We started to move our bodies as well as just our eyes. Charlie moved a few feet to his right to look into the kitchen area. I moved around the living room checking out an old dusty rocking chair that one of the rockers had long since been broken off from.

Jake opened an old rotting chest sitting near the cobweb covered fireplace. Finding nothing in it, he dropped the lid, causing dust to fly and also causing him to cough a little.

It surprised me that not three minutes ago we boys were contemplating leaving this place, afraid to even enter. Since we mustered up the courage to enter and finding nothing, our nerves had returned. This place was nothing more than an old abandoned house, nothing more nothing less.

Looking up, that fear we felt before we entered the house struck again freezing me in my tracks. "Didn't Mr. Knapp say they found Wanda hanging from the ceiling fan in the living room?" I asked, looking up at the old ceiling fan with the two broken fan blades.

The other two seemed to freeze in place when they looked up at the fan, too.

"That has to be it. That has to be the very fan she hung herself from. After all, this is the living room, isn't it?" Jake asked.

It took us a couple of seconds to rebuild our courage. It's not every day that three thirteen year old boy walked into a haunted house and finds the very thing that caused the house to get haunted.

When we did again muster up our courage, we decided to go upstairs, there wasn't much up there other than a bathroom with a broken sink. The broken piece found its way into the waterless commode.

We went into the last bedroom to check that out before we left the place as heroes, boys that conquered the famous haunted house.

Walking into the last bedroom, Charlie looked behind the closed door, slamming it shut as he did so causing the room to fill with dust.

Finding nothing in there, we pulled on the door to leave. For some reason it wouldn't open. We figured it had warped over the years. Charlie continued pulling on the door, when I noticed something that sent chills throughout my young body.

"Guys... Guys! Isn't this the room where we saw the curtain blowing out the window?" I asked.

Jake went over to the window, pulled the dingy curtain aside and looked out.

"Sure, this is the room. There is the front porch,," he said.

I believe that was the very second he realized why I asked the question in the first place because it looked to me as if all the blood drained out of his face. He seemed to be frozen in place looking at me, then to Charlie, back to me.

"What's wrong?" Charlie asked, moving over to look out the window. "I don't see anything out there."

I slowly raised my arm pointing at the window. "It's closed," I said. "How could the curtain blow out the window if it was closed? The glass isn't broken."

Just as Jake's did, the blood drain from Charlie's face. The smile he had only a few seconds before, was completely gone now, replaced by fear, fear I have never seen on his face before this day or any day after.

There were no words spoken among the three of us. Charlie ran for the door, giving it a jerk but nothing happened. I ran over to help him. We couldn't both grab hold of the doorknob, so I grabbed Charlie around the waist pulling on him as he pulled on the door. Still nothing! It seemed to be stuck good.

Again, we gave it a hard jerk. It seemed to give just a little, but then it snapped back into the same position, as if someone were on the other side of the door holding it closed.

I looked over at Jake. I wasn't sure, but it looked as if he had tears in his eyes.

Again, we pulled. Again, it would give just a little and then snap back, as if someone was on the other side of the door messing with us, having fun playing this little door game.

"Whoever is holding this door better let it go or I'll tell my mother!" Charlie screamed.

"You tell them, Charlie," I said.

The way the door acted, I was sure some kids must have followed us here and were on the other side of the door, just messing with us.

Just as we were about to pull on the door again, we heard glass breaking. Turning around, Jake picked up an old wooden slat that was once used in a bed frame and broke out the window. He stepped out onto the roof that coved the front porch and then jumped the few feet to the ground.

Charlie and I had absolutely no problem with that way out. We both headed for the window. Charlie beat me by a half step. As he was crawling out the window, he looked back at me. I saw a look on his face that scared the holy crap out of me when I saw him look toward the door. I turned around to take a look myself, before I also stepped out the window.

To my surprise, the door we were just pulling on with all our might just a second before, was standing wide open, just as we found it when we first came up the old stairs. To this day, I don't know if it was just a trick my mind played on me, or I really saw Wanda standing in the doorway smiling at me.

I do know this much: none of us boys ever went back to that house. When I was old enough to be able to date and drive, if I ever took a young lady parking, it was never, and I mean *never* anywhere close to that old house. You can pretty much bet neither did Jake or Charlie.

Chapter Seven

We boys had a pretty uneventful couple of weeks, playing softball workup, hanging around the park talking and just spending the night with one another.

Things really got back to normal when Gary and Bruce came back from the ranch with Bruce's Father.

One afternoon, right out of the blue Gary said, "Well I guess I will be moving to Chickasha as soon as we can find a place over there."

Talk about something taking us by surprise that sure took the wind out of our sails, Gary was one of us he would always be one of us.

"Why?" I asked, looking first to Gary then to each of the other boys.

"What?" Jake chimed in.

"Well, you guys know I live pretty close to a graveyard," Gary said.

That was an understatement; he lived less than a hundred yards from the little road that went around the graveyard that people used to drive on when they drove through the graveyard in order to pay respects to a departed loved one.

Gary lived so close to it that he had a hard time getting any of us boys to spend the night with him.

When you're a thirteen year-old boy, your parents tell you there is no such thing as a ghost; they tell you that there is nothing any different in the dark at night than in the light during the day.

You agree with them because first, they are your parents and your parents won't lie to you. Second, because they are your elders and you have always been taught to respect your elders.

However, how do they know there is no ghost? Is it because they have never seen one? Well, no one in my family has ever seen God that I am aware of, but there I am every Sunday praising God! The only person I know of that has seen God living in our town, is Mr. Gentry. But then, Mr. Gentry has also seen Santa Clause, as well as the Easter Bunny.

One afternoon, Mr. Gentry came over to where we boys were sitting in the park. He stood there for several minutes before he said, "Boys, did you know that the Easter Bunny is not pink like everyone thinks?"

None of us answered him; we only looked at him in confusion.

"Well boys, I was sitting smack on my front porch yesterday around noon, not bothering a single sole in this here world, when just as big as Dallas this here Easter Bunny comes around the corner of the house, hops himself right up on my porch and sits himself down on the empty flour bucket we keep there for extra seating,," he said to us just as if he had been talking with us for hours.

"That rabbit pure surprised me. I don't mind telling you,," he continued. "If I hadn't been so surprised seeing him sitting there on that bucket, I would have had a lot of questions to ask that bunny."

"Well, this rabbit tells me he wants me to spread the word that he is gray in color, not the pink color everyone seems to make him out to be," Mr. Gentry said to us.

"That rabbit seemed proud that I would take up this cause for him. Said it had been on his mind something awful, the way people treated him."

"The rabbit up and thanked me. Then, slick as a whistle, he hopped up off that bucket and left the same way he came, with not so much as a 'see you later.'" Finally, Mr. Gentry said, "That's why I'm here boys; I wanted to straighten out this color issue with you."

After he finished his little speech to us, he turned and walked away.

I asked my grandmother about Mr. Gentry that evening. She said he was a nut case. Said his mind was plum gone. "That boy has drunk so much whiskey that it's a pure wonder he has a brain cell left. People said his wife left him for her boss and moved to another town somewhere." My grandmother thought it might be Tulsa. "From that day on, all he wanted to do was drink. That's the reason he thinks he sees the people or things he says he sees."

After Mr. Gentry left, Gary got back to why his parents were moving to Chickasha. He said his family wasn't able to get any rest living where they live now. Said the last couple of months, older kids have started using the graveyard to do their parking and necking.

About the time the family got to sleep a bunch of kids would show up to park with their girlfriends, or sit on their hoods drinking beer and making complete fools of themselves.

Said his dad went over there once to run them off, but they just laughed at him. His dad was going to go back with a garden hoe to beat the fire out of all of them, however Gary's mother nixed that idea. She said the cops would be on him for beating a kid with a hoe handle.

I told my grandmother about Gary leaving town because of the kids messing around in the graveyard. She said best thing a person could do was hide behind one of them big headstones with a shotgun full or rock salt and shoot them in the butt with that a couple of times. Then, the next time they came to the graveyard would be in the back of Mr. Hansson's old funeral wagon.

It was hard for me to sleep thinking about Gary moving. That would leave a hole in our little group. I tossed and turned all night. Just as the morning light first started to appear, I came up with what I hoped would keep him in the group, keep him and his family in Verden.

The next afternoon I explained my plan to the others. They all seemed to think it might work. At least they were willing to try it; they were like me, willing to try anything if it meant keeping Gary with us.

We decided to put the plan into action Saturday night. We all made plans to spend the night with Gary. That surprised his mother. She knew it was hard enough to get one of Gary's friends to spend the night When Gary told her all of his friends would be spending the night, it surprised her, but she figured it was for moral support, one for all.

As the sun started to set, darkness set in we put our plan into action.

Charlie, Bruce, Jake and I did what we could to make ourselves look dead. We couldn't pull what we had in mind off if we looked like what we were thirteen year-old boys, still wet behind our ears, as granny liked to say every time she disagreed with me, which was most of the time.

Charlie and I used one of my mother's lipsticks. It had "Ruby Red" written on the bottom of it. I also brought along a plastic container of baby power.

I shook it first over Charlie's head, then had him close his eyes. I used the "Ruby Red" lipstick to color his eyelids. I also did the best I could to Ruby Red his lips. In the process of doing his lips, I gave a quick thank you that I was a boy. Putting this crap on was just that - crap.

In return Charlie made me up as best he could, only difference he made a long Ruby Red streak along my left cheek. Said it gave my look class.

I had a long white cotton nightgown that I just happened to find in my Mothers cedar chest. I knew she wouldn't miss it until the weather turned off cold again, or at least I hoped she wouldn't, because I was sure a thirteen year old trying to explain to his mother why he took one of her nightgowns wouldn't be all that easy.

Where Charlie came up with a pink nightgown with a big red bow about the size of a dinner plate, I will never know.

We decided not to put the nightgowns on until we reached the safety of the cemetery, to avoid anyone spotting us, something we would never be able to live down if that happened.

Just before dark, Charlie and I slipped through the fence to take up our positions a little north of where Gary said the kids did their partying and necking. Bruce and Jake slipped through, going a little to the south.

We waited behind a large tombstone that had, "Joseph Sheets Loving Husband and Father Born 1900 Died 1959, Carla Sheets Loving Wife and Mother, Born 1904." When Mrs. Sheets died was left blank.

"Look at this." Charlie said pointing at the name, Joseph Sheets, on the tombstone.

"What about it?" I asked.

"He died this year. Heck, he's really not all that dead yet. Only been here a short time." It wasn't all that hard to see Charlie was somewhere he really wasn't all that happy being.

"I have to admit, after that little trip to the haunted house that we made awhile back, didn't go so well, but being here wasn't my idea of a fun-filled Saturday night either.

All I could think to say back to Charlie was, "Believe me. He is dead. I don't think Mr. Hanson makes a habit of putting people under ground that are only just near dead. Now, shush."

We sat with our backs to the tombstone until it was completely dark. We were about ready to give up this idea when a shiny black 1957 Chevy pulled into the cemetery, coming to a stop not far from where we boys were sitting, behind Mr. Sheet's tombstone.

We didn't have any idea who was in the Chevy until the four kids climbed out. We knew one of the boys. He was a senior named Paul Compton the two girls names' were Dottie Davis, a junior, and Linda Dixon, another junior. We had never seen the boy driving the Chevy. We did hear the others call him Keith. We never did hear anyone say his last name.

From where we hid behind Mr. Sheet's tombstone, we could hear everything they were saying. They left the Chevy's lights on, which helped us watch them as well. They all had a quart of beer. Between drinking the beer, the girls laughing at whatever one of the boys would say (the way girls do) and Paul trying to get Dottie to kiss him (while Linda had no problem kissing the guy named Keith at all), they didn't have time to notice us.

I wasn't very experienced when it came to kissing. My experience was limited to my mother, grandmother, and a second cousin that kissed me on my mouth once, before I could stop her.

When Linda kissed Keith, I figured she would pass smooth out from lack of oxygen, because I didn't know anyone that could hold their breath that long, however didn't seem to bother her one little bit.

After they had been there around thirty minutes, Dottie needed to go to the bathroom. They told her to just go into the cemetery, pick one of the tombstones and do her business. She informed the others that wasn't just about to happen. She said that the only way she would do anything like that was if Linda were to go with her. She wasn't about to go alone. Paul said since he didn't have anything to do, he would be glad to go with her.

"Right. That will be the day,," s she answered, him laughing.

Charlie and I watched the young girls head off into the part of the cemetery that the lights from the Chevy weren't reaching. We could tell the beer they had been drinking must be doing something to them, because they seemed to not be able to stop giggling or laughing out loud.

I guess not just Dottie needed to use the bathroom, because both girls squatted down to do their business. I couldn't believe they were using someone's grave as their bathroom.

Charlie or I couldn't see what they were doing, however we had no problem hearing them desecrating some dead man or woman's grave.

Knowing this was our chance, probably our only chance, we slowly moved from one tombstone to the other until we were behind one the girls that were squatting behind a tombstone.

In the very scariest young female type voice I could come up with, I said "Please girls, please girls help me. Help me. I'm not dead. Please help me get out of here. Please! I won't hurt you."

As I peeked around the tombstone, I saw Dottie look at Linda and Linda look back at Dottie. I wished I could describe the expression on the young girls' faces. Dottie's mouth just fell open. Her eyes just shut completely, hearing my voice. Linda had the same expression on her face that Jake did the day he thought it would be funny to pee on the electric fence Mr. Morgan used to keep his two prize Holstein cows.

Both girls stood straight up. I also stood up in the moonlight and that was all it took. Linda started to scream at the top of her lungs. Dottie tried, but couldn't seem to get any sound to come out.

Together, they started to walk, run, back toward their dates. It was about the funniest sight Charlie and I ever saw: both girls doing their best to walk-run with their panties down around their ankles and their dresses flapping in the breeze.

The boys heard them scream and tried to meet them several feet from the car. They had a look of complete confusion on their faces when they headed toward the girls. I guess they saw Charlie and me standing in the darken cemetery, because they turned around before the girls got completely to them. The boys had run back to the car, jumped in and locked the two doors. Dottie and Linda had to bang on the car door screaming "Let us in, let us in assholes, let us in." Slowly the door opened just enough to let the two girls slide inside. The Chevy took off, throwing dust and gravel everywhere I felt sorry for Keith, somewhat, when he ran across one of the graves, striking the tombstone against the driver's side and causing a long gash that ran all along the side of the car.

As they were speeding away, Bruce and Jake stood off to the side of the road, just in their view, not close enough to them to be recognized, but close enough to be seen standing in the distance. The Chevy didn't speed up when the driver saw them standing between the many different tombstones, because the driver had the car floored by then anyway.

Gary's family never did move to Chickasha. We all hoped it was because of what we did that night. Lord knows, that was the talk of the town for several months. Kids completely stopped using the graveyard as a party spot. We hoped it was because of what we did, but more than likely it was the sign, "NO PERSON OR PERSONS IN THE GRAVE YARD AFTER DARK BY ORDER OF THE GRADY COUNTY SHERIFFS OFFICE."

More realistically, Gary's parents couldn't find a place they liked that met with the strict budget they were forced to live on. They had come to the conclusion that Chickasha was only eight miles away anyway. Gas was outrageous at twenty-five cents a gallon, but it was still cheaper to live in Verden than to drive to Chickasha when the need arose.

Chapter Eight

One morning, just after breakfast, I was standing on the front porch, just milling around. Milling around was what my grandmother called anything boys did when they weren't doing anything constructive. In her opinion, just about any time that boys were awake, they were milling around.

I was just about to step off the porch when Bruce came around the corner of the house in a heck of a dither.

"You got to help me. You got to. I've got myself in a heck of a lot of trouble, not trouble like the time I broke out Mr. Comb's window. That was just normal trouble. This is big time trouble,," he said to me, looking first one direction then the other, as if he was expecting the devil himself was about to come calling on him.

"What have you taken apart now?" I asked him, following his eyes around the yard as if I was expecting whatever or whoever he was expecting to show up.

Bruce had a bad habit of dismantling things. When his Mom bought a new vacuum cleaner from that door to door salesman, she kept it right by her side until Bruce's dad could put a double padlock on the closet door. She knew if Bruce was to get his hands on it, he would have it in pieces, trying to figure out what made it do what it did.

His folks owned a 1956 blue and white Ford coupe that his dad dearly loved. His dad even called it his baby. They didn't have a garage to put it in at night or during thunderstorms, so when a cloud would come up, Bruce's dad would drive his baby to the grain elevator, park it under the dumping bin to keep any hail from ruining the paint job, or worse, putting them small dents in his baby.

One afternoon, Bruce was milling around his porch when his dad drove up Walking up to the porch Bruce asked him how things were going. Apparently, his dad wasn't thinking when he said "okay, however I think the car is running a little rough."

Telling Bruce something was running a bit rough was like telling him Christmas was not December 25th. That it had been changed to that very day.

If his father hadn't been so tired from working a long shift at the elevator, he would never have said what he just said to his son.

When he got up from his nap, Bruce's dad walked out on the porch. There sat Bruce with the Ford's carburetor in his lap, pieces of it lying all around him.

There was no way anyone in Verden could put the carburetor back together. Bruce's dad had to have a local farmer pull his car to Chickasha with his old Case farm tractor.

All together, it cost his dad forty-five dollars.

He gave Bruce a whipping every evening after he got the car back for four days in a row. On the fifth day, Bruce was ready for the fifth spanking. He got it, but his dad didn't seem to put much effort into that one.

"Boy, I hope those spankings taught you a lesson. I know this may sound strange to you, but each time I gave you a spanking, I paid you for it. I paid you ten dollars each time I laid into you, then I deducted that ten from what it cost to have the car fixed. That last one was just a five dollar whooping. That's why it didn't hurt all that much. So now were even." Bruce's dad gave his son a hug when he told him that.

All Bruce could do was look up at his father, shake his head that he understood, and thank the Good Lord that the carburetor hadn't cost a lot more to repair, because he didn't think his butt would have stood up to it.

"If my dad finds out about this, I'm just a dead man, pure and simply a dead man." Bruce said looking down at me and still looking around at the same time.

"Well, what happened? It can't be all that bad," I answered him.

"Yesterday my dad taught me to take a metal coat hanger, straighten it out and put a hook on one end of it,," he said.

"And what was the reasoning behind that?" I asked.

"Chickens. You can take the coat hanger, walk up behind a chicken and grab one of its legs in the hook. Makes it as easy as pie to catch one," he answered.

Wow! I thought of all the many minutes, no it's actually hours if you put them all together, that I have spent chasing one of them stupid chickens for my grandmother. This had to be about the greatest thing ever. I made a mental note to do that with a coat hanger just as soon as possible.

"Then he showed me how to take that chicken, place it's head on the stump in the back yard and whack its head off with a hatchet," he said.

"Yuck! My grandmother does that. Thank goodness," I answered him.

"You should have seen that chicken. Just as soon as the critter lost its head, it went to flopping around, it jumped up for a few seconds running, falling first this way then that way, blood just squirting out of its neck just like that fountain over at the park. It wasn't cool, but it was about the most exciting thing I have ever seen in my life,," he said.

"Believe me when I say I know what people are talking about when they say running around like a chicken with its head cut off," he said.

"I sure hope when my time comes to be one of the dearly departed, I don't get up and run around like that chicken did,," he said with a concerned look on his face.

"I don't think you have no cause to worry. When a person dies, they just lay down," I answered him.

"So far, I haven't heard where the problem is," I said sitting down on the edge of the porch.

Sitting down beside me, he said," The thing is, I got so wrapped up in the whole chicken thing, when Dad took the chicken we killed in the house to clean, I caught another, chopped its head off, watched it do its running and falling-flopping around and then for some reason, I kept doing it until I had killed eleven chickens,," he said, looking me in the eyes.

I had no idea what to think about this. I have seen, I have even done, a lot in my thirteen years of life, but I had never heard of anything like this.

I knew there were a lot of people in the world that couldn't quit drinking. For that matter, there was a lot of those living right here in town. But, I had never heard of a person that couldn't stop killing chickens. As hard as I thought, I couldn't come up with anything that came close to a fellow that likes to chop off chicken heads to watch them run around headless.

A couple of year ago, I heard my mother talking to Mrs. Simpson about a man they caught in Lawton who killed several people. I sure hoped that guy didn't start out in life killing chickens.

"That's bad. Matter of fact, that's real bad." I said, moving over a little from Bruce, not sure how to take someone that got carried away killing chickens.

"I hate I did it. You know me. I have a problem killing anything. That is why I hate to go hunting with my dad,," he said, tears forming in his eyes.

He was right about that. I always thought he might just have a little sissy in him not wanting to go to the mill and shoot birds with the rest of us. Of all the guys, he had to be the one with the kindest heart out of us all.

"If I don't replace those chickens before my Father finds out, I am a dead man. He will just kill me and tell everyone in the family I joined the military or joined that carnival that comes to Chickasha each summer,," he said nervously.

I knew his dad would come apart like one of them fifty cent watches you buy at the five and dime. I also knew he wouldn't kill him. Might beat the fire out of him every day for the rest of his life however.

"Well we have to replace them before he finds out," I said in a matter of fact manner, hoping it would take a little worry, or at the very least a little pressure, off him.

"What type of chickens were they?" I asked.

"My dad called them Road Island Reds,," he answered.

"You leave them lying in the back yard or get rid of them?" I again asked.

"Well you can bet I didn't leave them lying around the yard. I may be a chicken murderer, but I sure as heck am not a stupid chicken murderer. I took them to the creek put them in that old rusted out car down there,," he said.

"Say, don't the Hogshooter's have them type of chickens?" I asked him.

I should have known better than to have asked that. The Hogshooters had all type of chickens. Sketter and his brother Benny Joe were known far and wide around Grady County as chicken thieves. They both flunked out of school way back before any of us boys were ever born. They tried their luck at making a living on the land their parents left to them, but with no equipment to work the land, or ambition, they decided becoming thieves would work out much better for them in the long run.

They first tried to become cattle thieves. The very first night they went out to steal a couple of cows, Benny Joe roped an old mother cow and was leading her back to the trailer they had stolen earlier, when all of a sudden Sketter went to screaming like a man gone crazy. In the moonless night, he had roped the farmer's prize bull, got his right arm and wrist tangled in the rope. The bull started dragging him around the field. It would drag him awhile then stop. Every time the bull would stop, Sketter would jump up trying to get the rope untangled. Soon as the bull saw him stand up, off he would go again. This happened several times before Sketter managed to get loose. When he got back to where Benny Joe was standing with the

70

Mother cow, he took the rope off her neck, walked around to the passenger side of the truck, got in said, "Let's go."

Benny Joe sat down beside him. Sketter looked at him and said, "Chickens. No cows. Chickens." From that day on the two brothers became the number one chicken thieves in the area. If someone came up with a chicken or two missing, you could just about bet Sketter and Benny Joe was mixed up in it someway or other.

The story goes, when they'd get a pick up load, they take them to Little Rock Arkansas and sell to a family that did business with the chicken processing plant.

People around here would pretty much just write the loss off, because the boys' father was always helping someone or other that happened to be in need. Mr. Hogshooter got himself wounded in the big war. The wound was so bad that he was never able to hold down a job for long, so the government gave him one hundred percent disability. It wasn't a lot, but enough for him and his boys to live on. When he passed away, the money stopped. The farm was paid for, so the boys just needed enough money to buy a little food and a lot of Falstaff beer.

I told Bruce to go get the other guys and meet me in the park. We would try to come up with a plan to replace the murdered chickens.

Jake thought we should just try to buy some off the Hogshooter's. Said he bet they would be more than glad to sell them to us and save themselves the drive to Arkansas.

We figured they would at the very least charge fifty cents apiece for a chicken. That added up to five dollars fifty cents. We added all the money we had between the five of us and came up with fourteen cents.

Gary asked if it would be stealing if we stole the chickens off the Hogshooter's if they had stolen them off someone else. It seemed like it wouldn't be stealing if they were stolen chickens anyway.

At lunch, I asked my grandmother if a person stole something that was already stolen, would that be stealing or not.

"Well, if this person that was stealing something back to give back to the person it was first stole from, than no, it wouldn't, but if they was stealing it to make a profit, than just as sure as the world is round, they are just as no account as whoever it was that started the stealing in the first place,," s she said, looking at me kind of strange.

When we boys met up again, I explained that since we weren't going to make a profit from the chickens, then it was okay if we stole them.

Just before noon, we met in front of the movie house. There was a Randolph Scott movie playing and we all wanted to see called Buchanan Rides Alone, but Bruce was one of our bunch. He needed our help, so the movie had to wait.

We crossed over the bridge, turned left on the dirt road and walked the mile that felt like two miles until we could see the old brown house the Hogshooter's lived in. We sat among some trees on a hill that overlooked the house for several minutes, wondering just how we were going to go about doing this.

Sketter was sitting under a large Pecan tree barking orders to Benny Joe. We couldn't make out what he was saying to him. We did hear the word "beer" a couple of times.

It was plain enough what they were talking about when Benny Joe came out carrying a galvanized tin wash tub filled with ice and brown colored bottles of something, When Sketter opened one, we knew it had to be beer. Looked like they planned to spend their afternoon not with Randolph Scott like we boys had planned, but getting snot slinging drunk under their old Pecan tree.

We sat there for what seemed like a couple of hours, watching the two men drinking. Sketter was the first of the two to lay his head back and stop moving. A couple of beers later, Benny Joe did the same.

We boys figured now was the best time. The two were fast asleep from all the beer, or even better, passed out from all the drinking over the last few days.

Another lucky break was the chicken coop was in the back of the house. If all went well when the Hogshooter's woke up, we would be long gone with the chickens.

We stayed in the trees as we moved toward the back of the house. We knew the two men were fast asleep. However, there was no reason to take any chances, chances we didn't have to take.

Seeing the coop, we all headed down the hill in a half run, half walk. Getting closer, we noticed an old rusted out model T Ford just inside the gate. This old car couldn't have been brought in through the gate. The chicken coop had to be built around it.

As Charlie took off the chain holding the screened in gate, I thought to myself this must be old Mr. Hogshooters car, something he must have been real proud of at one time. More than likely this was the car he drove around when he helped people. I guessed after his death the car must have broken down. Not having money to fix it, the boys' new enterprise, being chicken thieving, they just built the coop around it.

Bruce had made two coat hanger hooks. He used one. Jake used the other. Bruce would snag a chicken, bring it to me and I would then place it in one of the two brown gunnysacks we brought with us.

I never knew chickens could make so much noise. As they tried to avoid Jake and Bruce hooking them, a couple of them even flew over the five foot fence, and several flew up on the old car sitting on the steering wheel, the springs sticking out of the two seats. A couple of them flew up on top of the chicken coop itself.

The majority of them ran back inside the coop. I made up my mind right then and there holding that sack that I would start paying better attention in school, because anything would be better in life than stealing chickens.

It seemed like hours before we had eleven of the red ones in the two bags. As we turned to leave, we saw Benny Joe and Sketter sitting on an old worn tractor tire just outside the gate watching us. I know what my dog felt like when I caught him doing something wrong. It was the way I now felt as the two men stood up walked over to the gate.

"What yaw up to?" Sketter asked, looking at Jake then to Bruce.

We were caught. There was no other way to explain it other than we were caught. We really didn't have any other answer but to tell them we were stealing chickens.

I had no idea what these two men were capable of doing to us. Who's to know they may want to kill us, hide our bodies somewhere on the place, or at the very least beat the heck out of each one of us. So I decided to lie. I know one is not supposed to lie, but one is capable of just about anything when their life is on the line, just as I figured ours was.

"Well Mr. Sketter," I started to talk. "Bruce here has invented something he likes to call the Bruce rapid chicken catcher. We think it will become famous all around the world." I said, taking the coat hanger out of Jakes hand and holding it up for the two men to see.

"That's just a coat hanger you got there boy," Benny Joe said, smiling at me and turning to look at his brother.

"Gary, show him how easy it is to catch a chicken with this rapid chicken catcher," I said, looking at Gary.

Gary looked at me, then to Sketter, to Benny Joe, down at the coat hanger, then back at me. However, he seemed to be in kind of a trance, or daze being caught by these two unshaven coverall looking guys.

"Gary, catch a chicken." I said in more of a stern voice because he seemed frozen in place.

Gary seemed to come awake to what was going on around him. Turning, he walked over to where several chickens were pecking around at something on the ground. He stooped down, stretched out the coat hanger, then in one quick motion he had one caught. Pulling it toward him, he grabbed the chicken by its legs, holding it up above his head with an "I just won the prize" look on his face.

Sketter looked at Benny Joe, back to Gary holding the chicken up, back to Benny Joe, then to me.

"Wow, I never seen such a thing in all my entire life, and I'll tell you this much boys, I have had one strange life, but that there chicken catcher has to be about the best thing since them Mexicans came up with the idea to start frying their pinto beans before they went bad,," he said to us

"I love them refried beans," Benny Joe chimed in. "I like to mix the beans up with some rice, or even bread is good, refried beans darn near goes with anything, well almost anything. Doesn't go with okra. Course, I am not all that into okra anyways," he finished

To tell the truth, refried beans, okra, or any of the main food groups wasn't what was on our minds at the time.

"Mr. Sketter, Mr. Benny Joe we sure need these chickens. If you will let us have them, we will let you have all the rights to our chicken catcher," I said to him, as the others shook their heads, yes.

Sketter took hold of Benny Joe's old dingy white t-shirt, more or less pulling him over to the edge of the old coop. They talked for a couple of minutes. Well, Sketter talked while Benny Joe continually shook his head yes.

"What ya going to do with them bagged up chickens you got there?" Benny Joe asked pointing at the gunnysacks.

My mind started reeling trying to figure out what to lie about next. For one of the few times in my life, I couldn't come up with a story to cover our bagged up chickens. I just walked over to the tire they had been sitting on, watching us steeling the chickens they stole, sat down and told them the truth.

"Wow!" Sketter said." I sure know how it is to get ones butt plum smack into trouble. My dad was about the nicest man in the county, but if me or Benny Joe messed up, you can just about bet your last dollar that he would whoop the fire out of us. So you boy's take them chickens and get him out of trouble,," he said.

We replaced the chickens. Bruce thought his folks would sure as the world know the difference. The only difference was for a few days they didn't get as many eggs as usual.

Bruce's dad blamed that on the thunder storm that passed through a couple of days before, however, Bruce's dad blamed just about everything on thunder storms.

Chapter Nine

A couple of days after stealing all those chickens, Jake and I were sitting on my front porch, talking about, of all things, who in Verden cooked the best fried chicken. My grandmother won, however, that was just because we hadn't tasted everyone in town's fried chicken as yet.

Just as we were talking, Mr. Finchmoore came out his front door and walked to the mailbox, checking for a letter.

Walking back to his front porch, he looked over and smiled at us boys, then he motioned for us to come join him on his porch. I hesitated, knowing he would be getting into one of his long winded stories.

But I was sure my mother was cooking liver and onions for supper, so a long winded story was just what I needed to get away from eating liver. For the life of me, I could not figure why anyone in their right mind would want to eat that crap. Who in his or her right mind or had any sense would say "Look at that. Isn't it the liver? Why don't we cook that baby up?" Had to be one sick individual, one sick, hungry individual.

Sitting down on the edge of the porch, we looked up at Mr. Finchmoore sitting in his old chair. He asked, "Boys did you ever know when people first started wearing underpants, or even why underpants was invented?"

I knew he was about to tell us a cock and bull story that made no sense at all, well made no sense to us boys, but since he was getting along in age, I wasn't sure if it made sense to him. He might be getting a touch of that dementia my grandmother said about most the men in town.

If the grocer charged her a penny more than she thought he should, she would say the old cuss has gotten himself a bit of that dementia coming on. Onetime a fellow, along with his wife, stopped my grandmother and asked her if she knew where the bank was. "Fellow do you think you may be catching some of that dementia, because the bank is right there," she said, pointing across the street at the two double doors of the bank. When he made a u-turn she noticed the tag on his car was from Arizona. She was sure he had dementia then, coming all the way to Verden Oklahoma to cash a check.

"Well boys, best as I can figure, underpants was first used right after them pilgrim people landed somewhere here in America. Course it wasn't called America back in them days. I believe it was called something like Indian Country, or the New Land something or other like that. Makes no matter cause that isn't important one little bit about underpants."

"Boys, back in them pilgrim days, you couldn't get any food at grocery stores, mainly cause grocery stores hadn't been invented as yet," he said, looking off into the distance.

"No, back then, when you wanted food, you either had to get your gun and shoot whatever you could find.Rreckon back then, it was mighty easy to find about any critter you was looking for to shoot, being there wasn't much hunting went on for they got there, other than by the Indians, and I here tell they was more fond of buffalo than anything else. Sure, they ate other things, but buffalo to them was like a chicken fried steak is to us these days," he said, standing up and walking to the edge of the porch.

"Now, back then, they had lots of wheat and made lots of flour. You can make all kind of things with flour you know, biscuits, bread, pies, cakes such of things like that,," he said, sitting back down.

"Well, back then, women didn't have none of that cream they rubbed on their faces and body to make themselves soft, so what did they do? Well, having all that flour, they started using it to soften their skin. That's why when you see a picture of a woman back in those days, they look so white. It's the flour all over their face. In those days, women had to powder their bottoms 'cause of the heat, and yes, the cold," he said, looking into our eyes and leaning over trying to figure out our expressions.

I thought it sounded kind of farfetched, but it could be true. Course, I never heard one word about using flour in my history class. I did hear of them pilgrims growing a lot of wheat and such.

"Anyway boys, when a woman would pass gas, there would be a little white cloud, a flour cloud, or a cloud puff I guess you could call it. Their dress would kind of blow out in back as if there was one of them little fellows you see at the Chickasha Carnival under there, pushing that dress out. I guess them pilgrim women embarrassed real easy back then, so who caught the flack over it all? Sure enough, it was their husbands," he said, looking out over the yard.

"Anyways, the husbands got together for a town meeting. They had lots of town meetings in those days. When you're in a brand new country with nothing to do but hide from the Indians and grow corn, a town meeting isn't all that bad,," he said, turning and smiling at us.

"I'm sure all they did was stand around and tell farmer daughter jokes. Like I said, being a new country and all they didn't have no president, congress or the such, to be getting all worked up over, like the folks do now days,," he said, moving back over to his chair.

"So this one fellow came up with an idea to cut the legs off his sons knickers and let his wife wear them cut up knickers under her dress see if that helped solve the problem. I have to tell you for several days, maybe even a week or two, everyone in that little town of Boston watched that woman something awful. She couldn't go down to the corn patch or over to one of her friends' house for a pie, cooking, lots of pie cooking in those days, or could she go out to the outhouse to take care of her business without several people right behind her waiting on that little flower cloud to come popping out from under that dress,," he continued as he sat down.

Leaning over, getting as close to us as he could to make sure we didn't miss anything, he said, "Fact is, nothing, nothing at all came from under that dress. From that day on, every one of the women in that town started wearing knickers under their dresses. If they didn't have a son to borrow from, they made their own. I believe there is a statue of the man that came up with that idea somewhere in Boston right today," he said.

Scratching the back of his head and looking toward the depot, he said, "Now what was that old boy's name that came up with that underpants idea? Ho, yes, Leroy Panties." He smiled at us boys, got out of his chair opened the screen door and walked into the house. I'm not sure, but it sounded like he was laughing.

Chapter Ten

About two miles NW of Verden was a lake. We boy's didn't go out there all that much because of the distance, but when we did, we made a day of it.

The Saturday we decided to make the trip to the lake, we left early that morning; walking to the lake wasn't just walking to the lake. There were all types of distractions along the way.

About half a mile out of town lived an old man named Earl Peel. Mr. Peel was an old Navy veteran, and I was told he served aboard the USS Enterprise during the war. I don't know the complete story about him, just things I overheard from some of the old men around town.

I asked my grandmother if she knew him. For some reason, she didn't call him one of them "no accounts," like she did most all the other men in town.

She said something happened to him while he was at sea serving his country, fighting them little Japanese fellows. She said she believed he got some kind of a head injury. "Thank the Lord that the US Government is still taking care of him," she said. She was sure he wasn't able to work anymore, or would ever be able to work again.

She did say that whatever happened to his head made him do some mighty strange things. At times she believed his mind just up and left him, cause no one that had any resemblance of a mind would do the stuff that old veteran did.

We saw the smoke before we saw Mr. Peel's house. It was a large column of thick black smoke, and Bruce said when you see black smoke that means two things: something was still burning and whatever it was burning, had a body of some kind in it.

"Where in the world did you get that kind of information?" I asked him.

"I saw that on "Sky King" last week,," he answered

"Well "Sky King," or no "Sky King," that is a bunch of bull crap. If you see smoke there has to be a fire. Black smoke doesn't mean there is a body in it. It means something black is burning," I said.

When we walked past a large patch of cottonwood trees we saw the reason behind the smoke. There sat Mr. Peel , in an old red and white lawn chair next to several old tires he must have piled up to set fire to. He was wearing an old worn red ball cap, a yellow shirt he either cut half into or one that he must have gotten when he was in grade school, as it didn't come close to covering his big belly. He had on a pair of jeans he must have cut off when he was drunk as one leg was a good six inches longer than the other.

Beside him sat a blue and white water cooler with a beer along with a pack of weenies, a can of green beans and a small jar of mayonnaise sitting on top of it. Lying beside the chest was a couple packs of hotdog buns, and one onion.

"What in the world brought you boys out this way?" he asked .reaching over to take a weenie out of the pack on the ice chest.

"On our way to the lake," Charlie answered.

"Nice warm day for swimming," Mr. Pell said as he pushed the weenie onto a piece of what looked like to us was an old broken piece of fiberglass fishing pole. Then he held it over the fire.

"You boys want a hot dog? I got plenty iffin any of you want one," he pulled the one he was cooking back to see if it was done enough for him.

"Doesn't that old tire make them kind of taste bad?" I asked him.

"Well boys, it's like this, I lost my ability to taste anything a longtime ago, so it don't make any difference what it taste like. I can't taste it anyway. All my food kind of tastes like them little white cotton balls women use to do whatever it is they do with them,," he said.

"Heck, I had me a T-bone steak couple of days back. Other than it being a bit hard to chew, there was no taste whatsoever. Could have been eating a mud pie for that matter,," he said.

"You boys know you still have quite a ways to go before you make it to the lake,," he said

"Yes sir, we do. That's why we better be on our way," I answered.

"Tell you what I'll do," he started talking, looking first from one of us to the other, "If you boys will have a hot dog or two with me, sit and talk a spell we'll see if that old '55 Ford sitting right there will get you to the lake a lot faster than you walking. And you won't be near as tired when you get there."

"Sure" we all said in unison.

We boys didn't mind all that much walking, however, since walking had been our only mode of transportation since we learned to walk.

Walking down an Oklahoma dirt road in 1959 could be a magical experience for one thirteen year old boy's imagination, but when you put five boys together, their imaginations would run wild more often than not.

That small hill over there, or that large clearing in the trees could become an old Indian camp site where plans to attack a wagon train heading for points unknown were made, or it could have been a landing site for aliens from a far off planet that had been sent to Oklahoma to study our way of life.

No, we didn't mind the walk to the lake, but to get a ride would be even better. We would leave all the battlefields and the landing zones until our next adventure.

We sat around with Mr. Pell for about thirty or forty-five minutes, trying to eat one of his hot dogs.

I have made no bones about not liking liver. I think the stuff, more than not, tastes like crap. The texture is nothing but gross, however the hot dog I was trying to choke down right then and there was completely unfit for human consumption. It tasted like one of the old tires Mr. Peel was burning, with a dash of mustard. The only good thing about it was that the meat was a tiny bit softer than a tire. Because of that one difference, you didn't have to chew on it before you could swallow it, like you had to chew liver.

Charlie would eat just about anything. My grandmother always puts the leftover food she thinks is too old to be refrigerated in an old pail on the back porch for the neighbors old German Shepard. To me it looks like slop. Come to think of it, I guess that is just what it is - slop.

What is slop to one person might be something all-together different to another, because several times when we boys used the backdoor to leave, I saw Charlie reach into that old bucket and take out an old biscuit or a chicken leg with one bite gone out of it.

"That's for the Harris dog," I would tell him every time I seen him grab something out of the pail.

"Dog won't know I took it," was always his reply.

It wasn't as if he was not given enough to eat at home. His mother was a great cook, and all the times I ate with him and his family, it was like a mini-Thanksgiving. I think he just like to eat. It's a pure wonder he wasn't so fat, he had to stick out his arm so people could tell if he was rolling or walking.

I asked his mother if he ate a lot all his life.

"That boy has been eating like it is going out of style all his life. When he was nothing but a day or two old, he would completely dry up one of my tits. Have to switch to the other tit to keep the boy satisfied. Never seen nothing like it in all my days here on mother earth," she told me.

"I wasn't sure if I would be able to keep up with the little beggar. His dad and I thought we would have to run an ad in the Chickasha classifieds to try to find some girl that just had a baby and wanted to help tit-wean Charlie,," s she went on

"In fact, Charlie's dad went over to Chickasha to see what the charges would be to put an ad in the paper,," s she said.

"The editor of the paper darn near called the cops on him. Thought he was just your plain old run-of-the-mill pervert, trying to find some young girl around the area that would let him have at her. Said everyone in ear shot got to laughing something awful. The editor got just as red in the face as that shirt you have on, Sonny, 'cause he was so mad, being confronted by a real live pervert, that he went to screaming and thrashing around like he was about to go into one of them epileptic fits. Screaming about calling the cops and such. All Charlie's dad could do, was turn and run out of the place for dear life.

"For about a month, he wouldn't go back to Chickasha. He was afraid someone might see him and call the cops and him end up in jail just because he was trying to see to it his baby son got enough to eat and my tit got the needed rest it needs to resupply the milk it makes,," s she finished.

That was way more than I needed to hear. All she had to say was, "Yes, Charlie ate a lot." Bringing in the word "tit" to a thirteen year old boy was enough to stunt his growth from that day on.

"Well we sure need to get going Mr. Peel," I said

"You boys sure you don't want another hot dog, maybe a couple to take with you?" He asked.

My head, along with the others' heads went down. "No, no were good. No we're okay."

"Okay, then. Let me get the keys,," he said.

"Can you believe those hot dogs? I've never had road kill but I would as soon have that as eat another one of his dogs," Jake said, wiping his mouth.

"Quiet! Here he comes," Bruce said.

Walking up to us, holding the keys out, he said, "Okay, which one of you boys is driving?"

We boys looked at one another with a "What the heck do you mean who's driving?" mixed in with "Is this guy crazy or what?" look.

We thought all along he meant he would drive us. Not one of us had any idea he meant for us to use his car.

Before anyone could say anything, Gary said, "Oh, I guess I will drive. I was going to bring my mother's car but the carburetor lost all its traction going to the store, so I'll do it."

"Fine," Mr. Peel said, tossing the keys to Gary. "She is half full of gas, boys," he said. Then, just like that, he turned and headed back to the house.

"Let's go," Gary said, heading for the car.

Walking to the car, I had a bad feeling. It was the kind of feeling you got when a black cloud was hanging over your head. You know in your heart that this is wrong. Maybe "wrong" isn't the word I needed. Maybe the word was "bad." You know nothing good will come out of this. In fact, you know only bad will come from it. You can only hope, when you use the word "bad" that you don't end up using the word "real" in front of "bad," but I couldn't help it. This was going to be bad, REAL bad.

Gary climbed in behind the steering wheel as if it was something he had been doing all his life. Jake jumped in the front seat. Charlie, Bruce and I jumped in the backseat.

"Let's see now," Gary said, looking around

"Let's see now? What does 'Let's see now' mean?" Bruce asked.

"Don't confuse me. I've seen my Dad do this a lot of time. Just got to remember," Gary said.

I wanted to tell the others that we should just get the heck out of there before Gary gets this thing running and kills each and every last one of us. But, I knew we boys had taken an oath way back when we were in Miss Langston's first grade class, just like the Musketeers. One for all; all for one.

Over the years, I had lived to regret that "One for all; all for one." If things went as things usually went, I would live to regret it one more time.

What surprised me most wasn't that Mr. Peel gave us the keys to the car. What really surprised me the most, was as soon as he tossed them to Gary, he turned around and walked back to his house as if this was something he did each and every day.

Gary dickered around with the key until he got the car running.

"Piece of cake. Look at this little plastic piece right here on the steering column. It tells you what position you need to pull this lever into, to make the car go," he said. He turned to smile at Jake, and then back to us three.

"See this 'P' stands for 'park.' The 'R' means 'reverse' the 'N' means 'no.' I guess the 'no' is just something extra they put, 'cause it sure don't make no sense to have a 'no' on a car. The 'D,' now that's the important one because it means 'go.' Have no idea why they didn't just put a 'G' for 'go.' Course that's something only the folks that built the car know, I guess. Now this '1 2 3.' That's got to mean something, but for now all we need is the' D,'" he said. He had an "I just taught you guys something" look on his face.

We must have looked like a car with Mrs. Burgin in it. Mrs. Burgin was an old woman that drove around town in a 1955 Chevy. She could barely see over the dash board. To me, she looked just like a toddler trying to look over the top of her crib.

My grandmother said when Mrs. Burgin's mother was carrying her in her belly, something bad must have happened to her, making the baby stunt its growth. Grandmother said it could have been several things that caused the stunting. Could have just been walking down the street and a big dog snuck up behind her and scared the pee waling hell out of her. Could have been a million things that caused the stunting.

Gary pulled the lever into the 'D' position. "Ok now for the gas,," he said.

My head, along with all the other boys' heads jerked backward in such a violent way that I was sure my neck had been broken. If it was not broken, there had to be at least ten or fifteen vertebrae that had been cracked, or at the very least, now in the wrong position.

Gary didn't just push the gas pedal. He stomped on it, same as a fellow would stomp on a spider or a stinging scorpion.

I don't know if it says it in the Bible or not, but there are times a person has to scream in life. One is when he or she steps on a tack or nail, or when you walk into the chicken house, see a big old black snake lying there on the floor, or when you run face first into a real live dead ghost, or when you're sitting in the back seat of a '55 Ford as it goes around and around in the front yard of a house, out of control, with four other boys screaming at the top of their lungs.

Taking his foot off the pedal and grabbing the wheel, Gary got the car under control as best he could. Aiming it toward the dirt road, he stayed half on the driveway, the other half in the ditch. When the car hit the ditch, all five of us added another time to the list of when it's okay to scream. That's when you're in a car that hits a ditch. You feel your stomach slams into your tonsils.

Once we were on the level road heading toward the lake I looked over Gary's shoulder to see how fast we were going as it felt like he was going way to fast, the speed odometer said we were going about twenty-seven miles an hour, kind of hard to tell because he would give it a little gas then back off when he thought he might be going too fast, or so fast he might lose control put us in the bar ditch.

It only took about ten minutes before we got to the lake. Thinking we better not park the car where someone might see that it was just a bunch of boys driving, because they might think we stole the car, or worse, someone who might see us might also know my parents, or the other boys' parents. I had a good idea what would happen if my grandmother found out about this. If she did, I was sure I would get another trip to Hanson Funeral Home as the guest of honor. I would have company, however, because a nut or no nut, my grandmother would also put Mr. Peel in the funeral home for letting this happen with me, in the first place.

Pulling the car under a big cottonwood tree, Gary jerked the lever hard into "P." Again, I thought my neck was broken. When the car screamed to a stop, Jake's head hit the front windshield. When his face hit the window, it sounded just like when my grandmother got a good lick in on my bottom with the flyswatter.

The three of us that were sitting in the backseat flew forward, hitting the back of the front seat.

"My Lord, Gary, you near killed us all. You can't drive for squat," Bruce said.

"I got you boys here, didn't I?" he said.

When we got Jake's nose to stop bleeding, we all headed down to the dock area to swim.

Charlie, Gary and Jake jumped right into the water. Bruce and I just sat on the edge of the pier talking about Mr. Peel, the ride here, and what the ride would be like getting back.

Then, Connie Dycus and Marcy Samson walked past where Bruce and I were sitting. They didn't just jump into the water.

They waded in up to their knees, then just stood there talking, looking our way every few seconds. The boys in the water looked at them for a second or two, then went back to the horseplay they were involved in.

Bruce and I just sat there talking and looking at the two girls as much as possible without letting them know we were looking, but girls have a six sense or something about things like that. They know when a boy happens to be looking at them. It's as if girls have eyes in the back of their heads or else they have tiny little girl antennas, that alert them when boys look at them.

Connie and Marcy were two of the prettiest girls in our grade. We boys didn't care all that much about girls, however, each year seemed to change that just a little.

Looking at the two girls in their red and blue bathing suits kind of made the trip all worthwhile. Sure, there was a very good chance we boys would be killed or mangled so badly, only God himself would be able to recognize who we were on our drive back to Mr. Peel's house. However, sitting on this pier and looking at the girls, seemed to kind of make it not matter so much anymore.

"Go talk to them," Bruce said to me.

"Are you out of your mind? Why should I be the one to do that?" I asked him.

"Well, you're good at things like talking to girls. You have the girl gift,," he answered, smiling.

"Gift? I don't have no gift. Never had a gift to talk to girls, and I'm pretty sure I never will," I answered him, hitting him on his shoulder.

I would be a lot better at playing baseball or fishing. I'd be better at something I knew a little bit about. When it came to talking to girls, I knew nothing about it. Fact being, I didn't know much of anything about girls - period.

I knew older girls smelled good most of the time. Well, the younger older ones did anyways. The older girls that were married didn't smell at all. Well, with the exception of Phoebe Harris. Phoebe was a woman that had lived on South Main the last several years in an old rundown house. She refused to pay the city for water or trash pickup. The only time she showered was when she happened to be caught out in the rain. When she came to town to do some shopping, you could just about bet her smell drove the other customers out.

I asked Mr. Burger about girl smells one afternoon while at the depot. He said it was 'cause when girls reached a certain age, they started using chemicals to help attract boys. Said if a boy got a couple of sniffs of whatever chemical the girl was using, he was as good as a goner.

Said he had seen many young lad led down the path of sin as well as matrimony all because of chemicals.

"Take that Hanks boy. Just as fine a young fellow as there is in Oklahoma. Got a couple of sniffs of Julitte Barns' chemical and sure enough, he was a goner no more than a couple months after they met. Heck, I received an invitation in the mail requesting my presence at the First Baptist Church for that boys wedding," h

"Now, girls don't call them chemicals. No, they call it perfume, but if the truth be known, somewhere, I figure up 'round New York, Boston, someplace up yonder in the North, there is a factory run by all girls, and if a man was to believe in witches, I bet the head woman is a witch and that with and the other girls are putting them concoctions together," h

He said, "Reason I believe what I believe about witches and love chemicals and all, is because that Juliette Barns got one of the nicest boys in Verden. Hansom fellow he was. Had girls chasing after him like flies after dung. Anyway, poor old Juliette was nothing to be looking at. I hate to say ugly, but that poor girl would sure enough stop a clock. Her teeth were part buck teeth and part pushed in teeth. Sure enough the top teeth kind of pointed to the rear. When she smiled, the bottom teeth pointed toward whoever she was talking to," h

"Me and Ma Burger were attending the town picnic couple years ago. Well that poor girl got a ear of corn caught between her upper and lower teeth. Liked to never got it out. People got to thinking we might have to call the Ambulance out of Anadarko to fetch her to the hospital in order to get that ear of corn out of there. Finely all the tugging and jerking on that ear by several different people, it gave way just enough so a couple of men could jerk that sucker out of there.

"So you can't tell me that there isn't something in their so called perfume that makes a man louse up all the God given senses he has, boy, plum bad I tell you pure bad. So, if you happen to get a whiff of that stuff, you need to turn and skedaddle out of that area as fast as your legs will take you,," he finished.

We never did talk to the two girls. Seemed like sneaking a peek now and then was good enough. If the truth were known, I wouldn't have had a clue what to say in the first place.

What does a thirteen year old boy say to a thirteen year old girl in a bathing suit anyway? "Hi, I sure like your bathing suit makes your legs stand out real well."

I believe it's very likely impossible for a young boy, talking to a young girl wearing a swimming suit, to look at only her face, and it's a known fact if you look anywhere other than their eyes, it makes them mad as all get out. Again I don't know all that much about girls, but I would bet my last dollar, well if I had a last dollar, that girls kind of like you to look at other places, however I might be wrong about that, so best thing I can do is stay way away from them and hope whatever chemical they have on never reaches me.

We spent a lot longer at the lake than we should have. I guess it was because we had the car to make up a little time, not having to walk all the way back, however, when the sun started to set, we boys scrambled to get home.

I will have to give Gary his due: he did real well when we started back. I am sure everything would have gone along fine if there hadn't been a large watermelon patch along the south side of the road.

A watermelon patch to a young boy is almost as good as Ghost hunting, baseball, and fishing. It is something that just can't be passed up.

As we were creeping along Jake screamed out, "Watermelon patch, watermelon patch! Look guys, watermelons."

"Pull this thing over. Pull over man. Pull over!" Charlie screamed.

Gary pulled the car half in the ditch, other half on the road edge. Once the car was stopped, we boys piled out like the car like it was about to explode, like they explode in gangster movies. Then we headed for the watermelon patch.

Stealing watermelons was like a rite of passage for boys our age. After we climbed over the fence, we ran around each other, trying to grab the biggest one we could fine.

I found one that had to weigh at least fifty pounds, or at least it felt like fifty pounds to me. I almost never got it to the fence because I had to half carry, half roll it. When I made it to the fence at least the bottom wire was high enough that I could roll the melon under it. After Bruce put his in the car, he came back to help me carry mine to the car.

When we were all in the car, ready to make our escape from the scene of the watermelon heist, Gary turned to look at us. He also looked to see if anyone was coming out the back window. "Lord!" he screamed. When we boys turned around to look, we saw the same thing he saw: about a half mile away coming toward us was what appeared to be an Oklahoma Highway patrol car. All kinds of thing went through our heads, What if Mr. Peel called them told them we stole the car? Maybe they were just looking for watermelon thieves.

We knew we had to do something fast, as it looked as if the trooper would be on us in about one minute, if we estimated the cop's speed right.

They all looked to me, as if I was some kind of a wizard or something. What did they think I could do, make the trooper stop or turn around? Not likely.

"What?" I asked them.

"What should we do? Run, hide, what?" one of them asked. I have no clue which one asked as my mind was all caught up in what it would be like in jail. I was wondering if I would be doing my time in the small jail in Verden, or if they would take me to Chickasha to the county jail, or worse, would I end up in McAllester, where death row was.

I knew we had to do something and something fast, or our butts were in deep crap.

"Parking! Let's be parkers," I said to them.

"What? What the heck are parkers?," s someone from the bunch asked.

The idea came to me. I believe it was just like when our preacher said the Lord talked to him. At least it was a shot, in fact our only shot, at not becoming inmates.

"Gary move over next to Jake. Bruce you get down on the floor. I'll move next to Charlie. We'll act like we are a couple of boys with our dates, parking," I said to them

"You got to be out of your ever-loving mind. I would rather be put in jail for the rest of my life before I would ever plant a kiss on Jake," Gary said to me and to the others.

"You don't have to kiss him, stupid. It just has to look like your kissing him. Just make it look as if he is your date," I answered.

Jake slid down in the seat like he thought a girl on a date would; Charlie did the same in the backseat next to me.

"I hope you know where my hand is, Sonny, because you kiss me and you will be talking like a girl for the rest of your life," Charlie whispered to me just loud enough for the others to hear.

All the guys started to laugh, not out loud enough for the cop to hear, but loud enough for everyone in the car to hear.

"Tell your date to hold it down, Sonny," Bruce said from the floorboard.

"You'll think date if we get out of this mess. I'll find the biggest melon in the bunch and stick it where the sun doesn't shine," Charlie said to Bruce.

As the patrol car came over the small hump in the road, we went into our parking act. I made it look like I was kissing a girl in the back seat. Gary did the same in the front seat; I could tell the officer had slowed his car to a crawl as he got beside us. I didn't want to turn around to look at the officer because he might be able to see my ugly date, but I knew that I had to or he might expect something.

When I turned to look his way, I covered most of my face with my arm, hoping he wouldn't see just how young I was, because that would give everything away with just one look. He didn't seem to notice my age, he did smile at me and stick his thumb up showing approval.

When we saw his taillights at the intersection, Gary started the car slowly and pulled back onto the road. We made it back to Mr. Peel's house with no other incident. We left the watermelons with him with our thanks for letting us use the car. I also gave thanks to the Lord that today wasn't the day I would be meeting him in person.

The fun of stealing watermelons is not the eating of the melons; the fun is in the taking.

When I got home I was sure someone had called my grandmother told her about us and the car, but my luck held out because she wasn't waiting for me with a club or anything else to beat a child about the head and shoulders for doing something that child knew was wrong, real wrong.

Chapter Eleven

It had been a long tradition, not only for my small group of boys, but boys growing up in Verden as long as anyone could remember, when the five-thirty train came through town, we would stand by the tracks near the RR crossing sign on north main and wave at Mr. McNutt, the man driving the train. We boys believed he enjoyed it as much as we did, because several times he would throw pieces of butterscotch candy, gum and candy that was individually wrapped to the kids standing waving at him. He always had a big old smile on his face.

That all came to a sudden stop one Monday evening when the train came roaring through The guy driving was no longer Mr. McNutt, but some guy with a sour looking face or what looked to us as a sour looking face, because he didn't even turn to look at us standing there waving at him.

We asked Mr. Burger what happen to Mr. McNutt.

"Boys, Mr. McNutt retired. I bet he is sitting on some lake somewhere drinking something cold, with a big old fishing poll waiting for that big one to bite," h

"The engineer running the train now is a Mr. Bobby Reid, a nasty sort of cuss He doesn't seem to like anyone and a little footnote to that, no one seems to like him. The only reason he got the five-thirty run was because he married one of the big shots' daughter from Oklahoma City.

"I've been told that the main office just about has to threaten the conductors to work with him," he continued.

We boys thought that Mr. Reid would come around to our way of thinking if we just continued to go to the crossing for a few days, wave at him. We were sure that would make him smile and wave.

For five days straight, he didn't even look our way. Just acted as if no one was standing at the crossing waving at him, however, on the sixth day we could see him kind of leaning out the window. We knew he would come around sooner or later; this has to be the day.

When the train was right up next to us, we boys gave Mr. Reid the biggest wave ever. He looked at us boys standing at the crossing and stuck out his left hand, not to wave, but to stick out his middle finger at us, all while laughing.

"He just shot us the bird! The so and so just shot us the bird, the bird mind you," Charlie said in a not so happy voice.

We other boys just stood there with "what the heck" looks on our faces.

"I wish I had the gun my dad brought back from the war. I would make him wipe that smile off his face," Jake said to whoever was listing.

"Mr. Burger was right. I can see now why no one likes to work or even be around him," I said to the others.

You can't just shoot someone the bird like that, or at least you can't shoot us five boys the bird and not expect us to at least try something to get back at you.

Sure, he was driving a train that weighed millions or trillions of pounds, but millions or trillions of pounds wasn't near weight enough to stop us.

We decided to think about what we could do to get back at Mr. Reid for a couple of days. Whoever came up with the best plan, the others would follow.

Charlie being Charlie, he wanted to try to derail the train.

When we explained to him that a train weighing so much, first would more than not kill the conductor and Mr. Reid the engineer, not to mention all the people it would kill sliding through the town of Verden.

Bruce wanted all of us to load up on rocks, then when the train came by, to chunk the rocks at the engineer; he figured one of us was bound to hit him.

Jake was still for sneaking his dad's gun out of the house and take a shot or two as the train rolled by.

I really didn't have much myself; I was hoping one of the others might come through.

Bruce came up with the winner. He wanted to put people on the track for the train to hit. That would scare the crap out of Mr. Reid and if we were lucky it might get him fired as well.

He wanted a couple of us to walk on the tracks in front of the train and scare Mr. Reid enough that he would think he needed to stop the train see if he hit anyone.

I went along with the idea until I heard the part about stepping on the tracks. To me, that just didn't seem like a very good idea. No, that was a bad idea. If a person was to make a wrong judgment or if someone would fall or trip, that could really mess up their day.

After several "let's do this" or "let's do that," we all came up with the idea to make dummies and rig up some kind of a pulley to make the dummies stand up in front of the train just before it got there.

Gary and Jake went to work trying to rig up the pulley device to make the dummies stand up; Charlie and I were in charge of building the dummies.

We had a little help with that, because Mrs. Morrow had a scarecrow in her large garden that looked just like a young blond woman. We didn't figure she would mind us using the scarecrow for only the one afternoon.

Bruce took his sister's doll, the doll his sister loved so much even naming it Baby Kerry. He said he took it out of her bedroom closet. With luck, he would be able to get it back in there before she missed it.

He said whatever we did try, not to get Baby Kerry's pink dress dirty because that would give it away that someone had been messing with it. He said that his sister put so much pride in Baby Kerry's dress, if we got the least little bit of dirt on the dress then he would have heck to pay. He sure didn't want his folks to think he was playing with his sisters dolls. They might think him a sissy, or worse a pervert.

We made sure to be at the crossing each day to wave at Mr. Reid. Every day he still shot us the bird. Not even looking in our direction anymore, he would just stick his left arm out the little window and raise his middle finger.

We didn't tell Mr. Burger what we planned to do. We didn't know if he would approve or not, and we sure didn't want to get him in any kind of trouble with his higher ups because he was a good friend to us.

The day came that next Monday; we had Charlie hide behind a grain elevator about a hundred yards from the tracks. Charlie was holding onto a rope he planned to pull just as the train engine reached where we boys were standing, waving.

The train was right on time. About three hundred yards away, when we saw Mr. Reid's arm come out, we knew his middle finger would soon show itself and show itself it did. The finger popped up as the train reached our position, just as if it was a military exercise, we saw the scarecrow pop up holding Bruce's little sister's doll. The pink dress against the dark blue dress the scarecrow was wearing made it really easy to see.

When a freight train is just a few yards away from you ,it's almost impossible to hear anything but the rumble of the engine and the grinding of steel wheels on bare medal, however what we saw needed no sound. The engineer, Mr. Reid's mouth flew open as if someone snuck up behind him and poked him in the butt with a red hot poker.

I couldn't believe over all the noise we could still hear a shrill scream. To me it sounded like the time Mona Evens walked in the girl's bathroom at the baseball park and ran face to face with a five foot black garden snake. You could hear her scream all the way down by the funeral home. Our sheriff received several calls that day reporting a girl screaming. They thought it could be a possible murder, the way the screams sounded.

There was no need to worry about getting the little pink dress the doll was wearing dirty anymore. Come to find out a train hitting something going around thirty-five to forty miles an hour, destroys it completely. The head of the scarecrow went flying. Last I saw of it, the darn thing was flying over the grain elevator Charlie was hiding behind. Straw, pieces of clothing, doll parts flew every which way.

You could hear the brakes being applied to the train. You could see it, feel it trying to stop. Seemed like it took hours to stop because several cars went past us. Looking down the tracks, we were sure was about a mile, we saw four men running our way. They would stop about every other car climb under, look around and finding nothing, they would run down a few more cars while they repeated looking.

We boys thought it would be better to watch all the action from my front porch, which we did. Not because we were afraid, it was because we were scared to death.

We had no idea this would turn into such a big deal. Mr. Burger was out looking around the train. Several of the town's people were doing the same, a couple of Grady County deputy sheriffs even showed up to join the search.

After a couple hours, the train started to move again. That was an answer to our prayers as well because all we wanted by then was to get this fiasco behind us.

None of us left the safety of my porch. We felt like it was the safest place until all the towns folks had gone back to their jobs around town, or back to their homes.

The two deputies were the last to leave. They stood talking with Mr. Burger for several minutes. When they pulled out, Mr. Burger went back to the depot. Just before he opened the door to walk in, he turned and looked our way for several seconds. It looked to us like he was smiling. He was shaking his head back in forth. Of course, since we were such a distance away, it was kind of hard to tell. To me, it looked like it was a smile.

The next day we were at the crossing when the train came by. We figured if we weren't there someone might wonder why.

When the train got close, out came the arm. This time, the arm was holding a rag or something that resembled a rag. When Mr. Reid got next to us he let the rag go and gave us a big grin followed by a big old wave.

When we picked up the rag he was holding, it turned out to be a pink doll's dress all crumbled up and dirty.

From that day on if anyone of us, or anyone else, happened to be at the crossing when the five-thirty came by, they could expect Mr. Reid with a big old smile on his face.

Bruce was never caught taking his sisters doll, or at least he never let on that he did.

We felt bad about destroying Mrs. Morrow's scarecrow. We were going to build a new one for her and stick it in her garden some night, but the next time we walked by her house she had a new scarecrow.

Chapter Twelve

One morning as I was walking through town on my way to Jake's house, I saw two Grady County Sheriffs cars parked in front of the barbershop.

Being a thirteen year-old, I was sure they were still trying to find out information on that train incident.

Carl Fry was standing a few doors down from the barbershop. Being a kid with a very large imagination, I stopped and asked him, "Mr. Fry, what's the police doing here?"

"They've been told that there's a Peeping Tom doing some peeping in town,," he answered.

"Wow, a Peeping Tom in Verden!" I answered.

"Yes, just as sure as your standing there, it's a Peeping Tom," he answered.

"I had a pretty good idea what a Peeping Tom was, because if anyone walked by my grandmother's house after dark, she called him a no-account Peeping Tom. If they walked by in the daylight, they were just plain old no-accounts. Soon as the sun set, they turned into Peeping Tom no-accounts.

I asked her what a Peeping Tom was once.

She informed me, in no uncertain terms, that a Peeping Tom was a fellow that likes to hide in bushes or up in trees, trees with lots of leave of course so as not to be seen, then tries to look through windows to see what it is they can see without the person knowing they are being peeped on.

'Kind of like a spy, trying to get information, but in a Peeping Toms case, they were usually looking to see naked girl parts.

"They are not just no-accounts. They're just no good-for-nothing pervert no-accounts," s

I asked her if Peeping Toms were only men or were there girl Peeping Toms.

"Boy, Tom is a boy's name, no there isn't no such thing as a Peeping Tom girl. Why in the world would a girl hide in the bushes or climb a tree to spy in some window to see girl parts, when all they would have to do is stand straight up in front of a mirror naked? A standing girl could see all the girl parts they cared to see," she said.

"Well, how about the night they caught Susan Casselman looking in the window of LaDonna Huff's? Wouldn't you say that she was a Peeping Tom?" I asked.

"Nope, cause Susan wasn't there to see no naked girl parts. No, Susan was there to do a homicide. See boy, LaDonna Huff was a floozy. She wanted a man and she didn't care what man or who's man either, long as she got a man. Anyways, she got to trying to get Susan's husband, Alton, to come over so they could... How should I say this to you? Let me see. She wanted him to come over so they could put their things together,," s she said.

112

"Put their things together? You mean he brought his clothes and stuff?" I asked her.

"Just you never mind about that,," s she answered

"Anyways, Susan found out about it and it made her as mad as mad can get. She lit out that night to see if there was any truth to the stories going around town. Before she left, she put Alton's 22 pistol in her purse. She was ready to do a bit of homicide on the both of them if there was any truth to the rumors."

"I guess someone must have seen her lurking around the scrubs and called the sheriff's office. Thank the good Lord the police got there and took that gun away from her before she could kill the heck out of them,," s she continued.

"The rumors were only half true. LaDonna was trying to trap a man, only it wasn't Susan's man, Alton. No, it was guy named Tim, that only moved to Verden a couple of weeks before,," s she said

"I believe LaDonna and that Tim fellow moved to Little Rock but then who's to know. Once a no-account moves out of town ,you never hear from them again, and that just fine and dandy with me," s

"So LaDonna did get a man after all, so they could put their things together," I continued.

"Boy, what part of forgetting about putting their things together confused you?" she asked.

I figured there was more to this than she wanted to let on, but I knew I better not press her much more, because the fly swatter was sitting mighty close to her.

We boys have had dealings with goats, bull, chickens, even a grenade, but never a Peeping Tom. This was something that just couldn't be passed up.

It was decided we would catch this Peeping Tom, or at least find out who it was, then turn that information over to the sheriff's office. Who knows, there could even be a big reward in it for us.

There were five of us, so we decided if we split up at night, we could cover a big part of the town.

The splitting up was nixed pretty darn quickly once we realized that alone, there might not be a lot one person could do, however if there was two or more, one could run for help while the other watched the peeper.

It was decided that Jake and me would team up. Bruce, Gary and Charlie would team up as well.

That night just as the sun begin to set, our two groups started out. We had a good idea that we would find this fellow if we went around houses that had young pretty girls.

Jake and I decided to go over to Locust St., where the Cocker twins lived. The two Cocker girls were seniors at Verden High. I wasn't all that much of a judge of girls looks. Sure, I knew ugly. Ugly was pretty darn easy to spot, and pretty was just as easy, but the gray area was hard to understand. The gray area is the point between being called ugly and pretty.

That was the case with the Cocker girls. They was a long way from being ugly, but a guy couldn't call them pretty either.

I wasn't even sure if I was ugly or in my case nice looking. Many a time my grandmother told me I was so ugly when I was a baby, it hurt her to look at me.

Jake and I hid in some tall Johnson grass behind the Cocker house.

Bruce and his bunch decided to go to Morris Ave. That was where Connie Dycus lived. No one had a problem trying to decide if Connie was pretty. Most all the boys in school from the ninth grade up acted like sick puppies when she was around.

They hid in the ditch behind the old jail to wait and watch for the Peeping Tom.

Jake and I sat in that tall grass talking about baseball, like how Gary almost killed us with his driving, laughing under our breath as we talked, but mostly swatting mosquitoes. It felt like every mosquito in the area was in the grass with us.

Jake gave me a hush by putting his finger to his mouth, indicating for me to be quiet. Then he pointed to the bushes under one of the windows at the Cocker house. I'm sure I stopped breathing altogether. It's a wonder I didn't pass out waiting to see who was prowling around the house.

We waited and waited. I ended up taking short small breaths. When you're about to see your first Peeping Tom in action, you only breath in order not to pass out.

I had no idea what we would do when this peeper showed himself, because a thirteen year-old boy or even two thirteen-year old boys didn't have all that much of a chance with a full grown man, especially, a full grown man that has just gotten caught looking in a window trying to see naked woman parts.

The bushes moved again. Again my breathing stopped. I couldn't hear Jake breathing either. I was sure he was feeling exactly what I was feeling: excitement, fear, with a gut full of wondering who we would be catching.

You can only imagine what we felt when the Cocker's collie came out of the bushes we were watching. The collie looked across at the bushes we were in, then went up on the back porch and laid down.

We were in hopes that the other bunch was having better luck than we had. Jake and I called it a night. We decided to go home see if anyone in our perspective families had something for mosquito bites. Jake and I looked like we both had caught a bad case of Chicken Pox.

That Saturday night, we boys were not as enthusiastic as we were the first night. The mosquitoes were taking a toll on us. Our folks were getting kind of upset about us coming in a couple hours after dark.

Bruce's mother said she couldn't figure any reason, other than mischief, that would keep boys out a couple hours after dark. If she just happens to get wind of any mischief that we were involved in, she had no problem whatsoever whooping all five of us.

Jake and I went back to our hiding place in the Johnson grass behind the Cocker house again. The others went back to the Dycus house.

We thought about changing places and check out other houses, but we figured that our odds were better sticking with the same house.

There had been reports of a Peeping Tom in different areas. They were never the same place. That meant the peeper changed places each time he did his peeping. As small as Verden was, we knew he had to sooner than later show up at one of the places we were watching.

We had been watching the house for about an hour when the same bushes started to move again. I thought to myself, well here we go again. It's the darn old dog,

"Looks like the Cockers dog is messing around again," I said to Jake

"Looks like,," he answered in a whisper.

"No wait look," Jake said, pointing to a corner of the back porch.

116

Laying there in a corner of the porch was the collie.

Seeing the dog laying on the porch and the bushes moving under the window, there could have been every mosquito in Oklahoma land on us and we wouldn't have noticed, as excited as we were.

I sat next to Jake waiting and hoping this was the peeper. Our eyes were glued to the bushes under the window. There was some movement in the house, but we couldn't make out who it was because we could only see the shadow of a person through the curtain- covered window.

Then, all of a sudden, he was there looking into that same window. His head was just a few inches above the windowsill. It was just high enough for his eyes to look in.

We couldn't make out anything other than it was a man. That was for sure. His mannerisms or the way he crouched reminded me of someone. I didn't know who, but someone I knew.

Jake looked over at me shrugging his shoulders. Apparently, he didn't know who it was either.

We moved forward just a little, trying to get a better look, but we were still unable to recognize the peeper.

When the back porch light came on, the Peeping Tom turned and started running in our direction. When he got under the streetlight, about a block away, both Jake and I recognized him at the sometime. It was Sketter, Sketter the chicken thief.

Sketter of all people. We were sure if the peeping tom was from Verden, we would know him, but Sketter, Sketter of all people. We thought all he did was sneak around stealing chickens. We thought that, when not stealing chickens, they were just sitting around drinking beer.

We boys figured Sketter got to sitting around thinking to himself one afternoon or evening, and came up with the thought, "Wow, there has to be something in life I would like to do besides being a beer-drinking chicken-thief."

We figured he might have decided it was time for him to take up dating. Not knowing all that much about women, he must have decided to do a little window peeking to find out what, if anything, he could about women.

Charlie said he thought Sketter could peek in every window in town trying to figure out about women, but when it came right down to the nut cutting, he had no idea who would even think about going on a date with old Sketter.

Sketter wore the same old pair of overalls all the time. Charlie figured the only time them overalls got washed was when he got caught out in the rain, or if he happened to fall in the river, drunk while fishing.

There was a hole about the size of Mason jar lid in both sides of his butt. The holes were just large enough so you could see what used to be his white underwear, that were now his brown underwear.

The Peeping Tom being Sketter presented a problem to us boys. Since we knew who it was, we figured if we didn't tell the police and later someone found out we knew, we could get in trouble for not telling.

On the other hand, if we told and Sketter found out we told, he just might tell about the chickens we tried to steal from him.

We knew we had to do something, because it just wasn't right to let some fellow peek in windows trying to see naked girls.

As luck would have it, we boys were walking through town heading to the fishing spot where the angel struck the water with his staff, when we saw Sketter come out of the store, caring a bag of chicken feed.

I turned to the others and said, "Okay guys, play along."

"What's up boys?" Sketter asked.

"Nothing much. Going to the river to do a little fishing," I answered him

"Those chickens work out okay? Did they get the boy out of trouble?" he asked, looking at Gary.

"Yes sir, it all worked out like we hoped it would," I answered.

"Say, did you hear there is a Peeping Tom been hanging around town? Got the girls plum scare to death!" I said to him, acting like I was about to walk away.

"Peeping Tom! You mean one of them people that peek into houses without folks knowing?," he asked.

"Yes, Mr. Sketter, but they will have him caught in no time now. They got a couple hundred Army guys from Ft. Sill to come over and stake out every house. The sheriff said there was no reason to arrest this person, whoever it might be. Sheriff said he was just going to take him to the river."

"The river! Good gosh, why would he take him to the river?" Sketter asked. You could see the concern in his eyes, yet he was trying to act like it really didn't matter to him.

"Well, the way I heard it, the sheriff is keeping a tally of all the houses that people said he peeped into. So far it is up to forty-six."

"Forty-six! There must be some kind of mistake. I heard it's more like four,," he answered in a high voice.

You could tell we had him worried. I had just picked the number forty-six out of the sky. It just seemed like a nice fine number to me.

"I don't think there are forty-six houses in this town,," s ketter said.

"Don't know about that. I just know they plan on taking him to the river, tie him to a tree and give him a lash for each house. That would be forty-six lashes he would be getting. Then the sheriff said he planned to make this fellow walk from North Boundary St., down North Main Street, across the tracks, then down South Main to Highland Ave naked as the day he was born."

"Can the Sheriff make a fellow do that kind of thing?" he asked, in more of a whisper this time.

"You have had dealings with the Sheriff before haven't you?" I asked him.

"Sure, I have several times, but all he did was lock me up for a day or so, let me pay the twenty-five dollars fine then let me go,," he answered, visibly shaken.

"Well, there won't be no twenty-five dollar fine for this peeping guy," I said to him.

"I also heard that they may make whoever it is pay for all the Army guys that is coming to catch the peeping guy," I said.

"Well, that would be too bad. Well, what I mean is that would be too bad for the Peeping Tom, or I don't meant too bad, I mean that would be good. Serve him right doing that sort of thing," Sketter said, turning and walking away a little faster than we had ever seen him walk before.

I guess what we said to him kind of put the fear of God into him because there were no more reports of Peeping Toms in the area, well, other than old lady Householder.

Miss. Householder lived on First Street. She was born in that house; raised in it, and after all her family died, she continued to live in it. My grandmother said she was around

120

ninety years old and never been married. In fact, my grandmother wasn't sure if she had ever had a boyfriend.

She said a lot of people thought she was a lesbian, but my grandmother said that was just a bunch of horse poop. The real reason was, she was just a natural fearful woman, scared to death of about anything.

Granny told me a fellow come down from somewhere like Illinois or Ohio; she wasn't real sure where the fellow was from. Anyways, he was on his way to Rush Springs to pick up a load of watermelons to take back with him to sell up there and make a little extra pocket money.

"Apparently he had some reason to stop in Verden. Who knows why. Maybe to pick up a pack of Cigarettes, use the bathroom. Didn't make any difference why he stopped here. The point was, he ran into Miss Householder in the store and took a real fancy to her right there next to the rabbit and chicken feed," My grandmother told me.

"The story went, he watched her several minutes, picking up this and that. When she pushed her cart down the aisle he was standing in, then he apparently said something like, "Hi Miss, or is it Mrs.?"" Granny continued with her story.

"That was all it took for Wanda Householder to freak out. She looked up at him, let out a scream that could be heard across the street inside the bank with the bank doors closed. She turned and ran for the doors. No one saw her after that for around three, maybe four years. Whenever she needed something from the store, she had it delivered. Caused the delivery boy to quit, because no matter what she bought, be it two dollars worth or fifty dollars worth, she always gave the delivery boy a five cent tip, no more no less, always five cents, after he walked the nine blocks to her house one-way," she said.

"From that day on Miss Householder called the sheriff if the street light on the corner happened to go out, or dogs walked across her yard. Where there is a dog, there is a dog's master, she told the sheriff. If a man happened to walk down the sidewalk in front of her house, she would call, always the same, reporting that a Peeping Tom rapist was outside her door. She called four five times a week. One month in March, she called every night two or three times. On Halloween the sheriff sent a car to her house to keep her from freaking out and completely ending up in the Chickasha Hospital with a heart attack,," s Granny said, laughing.

"I don't mean to make fun of the old woman. I guess she must have one of them phobias you hear about these days. God himself might have it in his mind to lay a phobia on me for funning about her, but a body can't help having a little fun,," s she said.

"Phobias. What's a phobia?" I asked her.

"I got no time to be explaining such things with you right now, boy. Got to get to cooking if there is going to be any supper served around here this evening,," s she said.

One thing about my grandmother, if she didn't want to talk about something, the kitchen always gave her an excuse to get out of it.

That word phobia had me puzzled. I figured if anyone knew about it, it would be Mr. Finchmoor.

I walked next door and knocked on his door. I knew I would have to knock a couple of times because he always had to peek out the window to see who it was.

He told me one day, he had no use for them people that dress up real nice and come to your door, trying to get you to join their church.

"Now don't get me wrong. I'm a God fearing man. Well, a God fearing man most the time. I may stay off the straight and narrow now and then,," he said.

About the third time I knocked, he came to the door, pushed the screen open and asked me, "What brings you here, Sonny?"

I explained to him about what my grandmother had said about phobias. Wanted to know if he knew anything about phobias.

"Tell you what, I don't know everything about everything, but I know a little bit about everything,," he said.

"Have a seat. I'll be right out,," he said.

In a couple of minutes, he was carrying two coke colas that he had gotten and, handed me one. He sat next to me in the other old white chair he kept on the porch.

"Now let me see, I do recollect a little about some phobias. You might not know it, but I have an Uncle Clarence Finchmoore that was married to a woman that had been married before she married my uncle. Well, she had a daughter. I believe her name was Tamara," he said, taking a drink from his bottle.

"Now, that girl had a couple of them phobias. One was Anablephobia, which was the fear of looking up. Her mother tried about everything in the world to cure the girl of that she bought her one of them straw hats that had that little green visor sewed right into the brim," he said.

"That hat did the poor girl not one bit of good. When they were walking around, a person was hard pressed to see

Tamara's face, her keeping her head down as she did. Just about have to squat down to look up at the girl," he said, holding the bottle up see how much coke he had left.

"Was no way Tamara could ever go anyplace by her lonesome. Poor thing would get lost, her not ever looking up to see where she was. I was told before the Anablephobia overtook her completely, they sent her to the store for some collard greens or something green anyways. When they found her, she was walking east on Highway Sixty-two, about halfway to Chickasha,," he said, taking the last drink out of his bottle.

"From that day on, if she ever left the house, her mom or dad went with her," he said, sitting the empty bottle on the floor.

"Everything was all well and good until she started showing signs of also having what the doctor called Hypnophobia. Boy, that's being afraid of sleeping as well as being afraid of being hypnotized. Since you don't run into many fellers that hypnotizes people all that much, her folks didn't worry a lot about the hypnotizing part of her phobias. That pretty much took care of itself,," he said, leaning back in chair.

"But that sleep thing just about drove her folk's plum up the wall, since she didn't sleep much. She stayed up most all the night, milling around the house, bumping into this and that, since she wouldn't look up. More than once, she walked into her parents' bedroom, bumping into their bed, sometimes just falling right smack on top of them. I was told it scared her dad so bad, early one morning that he lost every bit of control he had over his bladder. They wasn't able to sleep in their bed for several months after that. They ended up making a pallet on the living room floor. They had to put the mattress outside by the garden until the smell got out of it enough for them to again sleep on it," Mr. Finchmoore said.

"One thing about Tamara and her parents, they were sure enough church goers. When the doors opened on the Free Hope and Love Baptist Church, they were sitting on the front row, or as near to the front row as they could get,," he said

"If you were to ask me, I figured they attended church so much, in hopes God would kind of take pity on Tamara, reach down from the sky and cure her,," he said

"Like every Preacher in the entire world says, God works his miracles in his own time, course most people don't abide by that they keep pestering God hoping he will get right to them. ' He said smiling down at me.

"Then when God does work a miracle most people are blinded by what they wanted and not what they ended up getting, not seeing they done got themselves a different miracle, a better miracle than the one they was asking for in the first place."He said sitting back down.

"People are strange birds that way," he said.

"That was kind of the way it was in Tamara's case I am sure. I bet they were always in Church sitting watching the Preacher walking around Bible over his head screaming about damnation and hellfire, the Finchmoore's not paying one little bit of attention to the Preacher scream a dancing around up there, the three of them was praying for Tamara to get a little relief from her fear of looking up as well as that fear of sleep," he said sitting back down.

"Un be known to them a miracle was taking place right there in that Church no more than three or four pews behind them, no sir it wasn't the miracle they were praying for, no sir not that miracle at all, but you can bet your life it was a card carrying miracle taking place," he said, looking to me than out toward the depot.

"You see there was this young fellow, I believe his name was Eric Lunday. Every time the Finchmoore's was in that church praying, he was in there as well," he said, still looking out across the tracks.

"Seems Eric wasn't in there to watch that Baptist preacher either. No, he had taken a shine to Tamara way back in high school. He just didn't have the courage to talk to her. So, he just sat in church day after day, just loving Tamara from afar," he said.

"Well, one Wednesday evening, the church was having a social, and yes before you ask, they were there a praying for some relief for their daughter's problem, before everyone sat down to eat and gossip about Catholics or any other denomination that didn't happen to be Baptist. When the Finchmoore's finished trying to persuade the Lord to hurry with the miracle, the three of them sat down at the table to eat." Mr. Finchmoore said.

"Right then and there, their miracle happened over plates of fried chicken and potato salad. Eric went over to Mr. Finchmoore, knelt down by his chair and just as big as big could be, he said, 'Sir I would very much like to court your daughter Tamara.' Tamara was sitting next to her father and heard him ask to court her. Since he was kneeling down, she got a good look at him. She poked her farther in the ribs to get his attention. When he looked at his daughter, she was shaking her head yes as best she could, having Anablephobia, however, he got the point right off the bat and told the boy that since he asked in the right proper way, he would be glad to have him come calling on his daughter," Mr. Finchmoore said to me.

"Sometime during the social, Mr. Finchmoore took Eric to the side and explained to him about her fear of looking up. Said if he took her to the movie show, the park and such, he had to stay right by her side as she had the tendencies to wander off," he said

"Apparently Tamara wasn't the only one that had phobias. Seemed Eric had Placopiobia or the fear of tombstones. Said that was what brought him to church in the first place. Several of his family members had passed on to their glory and he wanted to go to the cemetery with flowers and pay his respect, but when he got near the cemetery gate, seeing all them tombstones sent him into a pure panic. He never was able to put flowers on any of his loved ones graves. He didn't even come out of the house on Memorial Day because he felt so guilty. That's why he was always in church to pray for all his family buried up on the hill, as well as look at Tamara," he said again, smiling at me.

"Those two kids hit it right off. When Eric went calling on Tamara, he always took a pair of plastic pink, fur lined handcuffs he found at a novelty store in Chickasha. They must have been a pure site walking down the street or going into the picture show handcuffed together," he said, smiling and acting like he knew something he wasn't about to tell me.

"Now boy, I know what's on your mind the way you are looking at me. Why would he take her to the picture show if she was afraid to look up, because she couldn't see the picture?" he said.

"Well Eric was a very, how should I say this, ingenious lad. He took the mirror his mother used to check her hair. When Tamara sat there, all she had to do was watch the movie as it reflected off the mirror. Sure if there was any writing on the screen it was backward in the mirror, but that didn't seem to matter to the two kids," Mr. Finchmoore said.

"They courted for about six to eight months 'for Eric got enough cods to ask her to marry him," Mr. Finchmoore went on.

"Being the polite young man he was, he asked Mr. and Mrs. Finchmoore one evening after eating a chicken and dumpling dinner with the family. Apparently Tamara told Eric that his dad would agree to most anything after eating his fill of chicken and dumplings," he said, standing up again.

"When the folks heard he wanted to marry their daughter, you would have thought they had been visited by the good Lord his very self. It wasn't that they didn't love their daughter. No sir, they loved that girl a fearsome amount, but you got to admit it had to come as a relief to them that they no longer had to lead her around town with her head down, or wake up in the middle of the night her falling on them because she was afraid to sleep. So they said yes faster than a chicken will eat a June bug.

"What is miraculous about all this is, after the wedding, them kids got themselves the honeymoon suite at the Hotel Black in Oklahoma City. The very next day after the honeymoon, when they came home, Tamara was no longer afraid to look up. She done went and lost her Anablephobia, and I been told she slept like a baby from then on. I have no idea what happened on their honeymoon night. Whatever happened must have done in all those phobias from them two kids, because every Memorial Day you can see them up to Fairlawn Cemetery placing flowers on family graves, "he finished.

I wasn't sure if everything he told me was on the up and up, the way he liked to embellish stories, but I did learn that phobias were the fear of something or other.

Chapter Thirteen

Charlie showed up at my home about six o'clock one Saturday morning. I knew he had something on his mind, because during the summer his mother said it just about took an act of Congress to get him out of bed before noon.

Apparently, a couple of the senior boys had given him a hard time the day before while he was walking past the pool hall. I guess they made fun of him in his mussel shirt. Charlie could have put up with their teasing with no problem if only there hadn't been a couple of girls with them.

All of us boys tease and get teased, but there is a difference between teasing a person and embarrassing someone. The boys took their teasing to the point it embarrassed him. He wanted to punch the older boy in the face, but that would be like walking up behind a bull and slapping in on it privates, something he knew all about from last summer.

While he was telling me the story, we thought we would walk over to the depot to see what was going on.

Sitting around there talking to him, the subject came up about the boys embarrassing him on their way to the pond to go swimming with their girlfriends.

"Are they swimming right now?" Mr. Burger asked.

"They said they were going today. First, however, they were going to the store to pick up stuff to have a picnic lunch. I overheard one of them say their plans were to go around two or two-thirty," he answered.

"Who were these kids anyway?" I asked.

"The two boys were seniors. One of them was Jeffrey Hines. The other one was Merle Jay. The two girls, I'm not real sure about, but I believe the blond girl was Kerrie James, and the other was Debra Jensen," Charlie said.

"I know them two boys. They are ornery as the dickens. Last Christmas they murdered Santa. Then on Halloween, they were the little cusses that put that bag of poop on my porch, lit it on fire and knocked on my door, hoping I would come out and stomp it out. That didn't work. I didn't just get off that turnip wagon you know, " he said.

"What do you mean murdered Santa?" I asked him.

"I'm not talking about the flesh and blood Santa; no, I'm talking about the plastic Santa it takes me about an hour to blow up. The boys came over a few days before Christmas with a couple of butcher knives that I figure they stole from their mother's kitchen. They went to stabbing my Santa like a couple of crazy hoodlums. Now that I think about it, that's just what they are, a couple of hoodlums," he said.

"Wow!" I answered.

"Anyways, to put the icing on the cake, they took off they kicked the red nose off Rudolph. Now, I want to ask you plain

132

and simple, is Rudolph any good without that little red nose of his?" he asked.

"Now when Christmas comes, I have nothing to put in my front yard, except my broken Rudolph. Can't get the Christmas spirit with a broken Rudolph," he continued

"Well boys, you're in luck. I got just the thing for you, if in you can get out to the pond before they do, you can fix their wagon, and fix it good," he said, walking into the room that had a lot of big batteries. He opened a closet and took out something about the size of a half round lunch box. Walking over to us, he said, "Here she is."

I never saw anything like it before. It was made out of medal and had what looked like a crank on the end of it.

"What is that thing?" Charlie asked him.

"Boys, that is a telephone, pure and simple, just a plain old telephone," he said, sitting back down in his chair.

Charlie was turning it this way and that, trying to figure if you talked into it or what.

"I've see a lot of telephones in my life, but never a telephone like that," I said

"What are these two long wires for?" Charlie asked.

The wires were about twenty-five feet long each.

"Here, let me show you how it works. Sonny, you take hold of the two wires. Put one in each hand and stretch them out as far as you can," he said.

When I had the wires stretched all the way out, he said to Charlie. "Okay Charlie, turn that little crank as fast as you can."

When Charlie started spinning the crank, an electric shock hit me so hard, I thought I was going to not only pee myself, but lose control of my bowls as well. I tried to let go of the wires but the electric shock going through me was in control of every part of my body but my mind and the feeling of being shocked.

Soon as Charlie stopped turning the crank, it stopped shocking me.

"Crap! Crap, what is that thing?" I asked throwing the wires on the floor, now that I was once again in control of my body.

"Boys, this thing is what people use to fish with. They throw the leads or wires into the water, turn the crank sending an eclectic charge into the water, and shock the fish which come floating to the top of the water," he said with a big old grin.

"Then all you have to do is wade or swim out and pick up the fish, If the fish are too small to keep, or you get more than you need, the other ones will soon get over the shock and take off swimming like nothing ever happen," he said.

"Now, if a person was to place these wires in a pool kids use to swim in, I would say those kids might get the shock of their lives, if you know what I mean," he said to Charlie.

"Can we borrow this thing for the day?" I asked.

"Well, I don't see why not," he answered

As we were about to leave he said, "By the way, don't let the game warden catch you with that, because it's against the law to shock fish," he said, laughing as he closed the depot door.

Being against the law put a little damper on having it, but what we had planned to do with it out weighed anything else.

After we left the depot, we headed to the other guys' houses and informed them what was going on with the senior boys and what we planned to do with the telephone.

One thing our little group did was stick together, so the five of us headed for the large pond the town kids used as a swimming hole if they couldn't get to Chickasha, to their large swimming pool.

When we got to the pool, we were in luck, because there was no one else around. Kind of strange for the summer.

Charlie wadded out with the two wire leads, placing them a few feet apart.

We sat up behind some tall weeds on the shore to wait.

A couple girls we didn't know showed up, wadded out to about knee deep in the water, looked around, but seeing no one else, they left.

Jake said he figured since there was no boys around they could flirt with, they thought what the heck and left. Girls don't care all that much about swimming anyway because it makes their make-up run, causes their hair to go straight. Before a girl would go through all that, they just about have to have a boy around.

"How do you know so much about what girls think and do?" I asked him.

"I like to study on things. Girls just happen to be fun to study on, I guess," he said.

"Well, to tell the truth, girls are really hard to second guess. You think you have one all figured out, then just like that, she does something completely unexpected," he said.

"Take that Sandra Best, everyone thought she was in love with Jerry Waddel. She was always walking around with him. She even ate at the Waddel house lots of times. People around town talked about how nice a couple they made. Figured they would get married," he said.

"But when Jerry asked her to get married, he found out she didn't care all that much for him. It was his sister she liked all along. It 'bout done old Jerry in. I figured because all the money he put out on her taking her places like the movies, trips to Anadarko and Chickasha to shop, not to mention all the times he took her to different restaurants on them shopping trips, a man don't like investing all that money in a girl if in he don't have plans to start a family," Jake said.

"Tell you what, if I ever get to liking a girl and decide I want to take one out, I will lay my cards right there on the table. I'll tell her something like, 'Say now, look here, I got me some plans to get married to you one day. If you don't feel the same, then we best call this off, because the girl I will end up getting married to might not like me spending money on you,'" he said to us.

"Well good luck with that," Bruce said.

About that time, we heard a car pulling up. All five boys hunkered down, not wanting to be seen until they saw who was pulling into the area.

We couldn't see the car as hard as we tried, because they parked in the trees on the other side of the pond.

Before anyone came into sight, the boys recognized the voices to be that of the young people that gave Charlie such a hard time.

Charlie whispered to the others, "That's them. I recognize Jeffrey's voice."

It would have been a scary sight to Jeffrey and his friends, if not a funny sight, seeing our five faces peeking out from under the tall weeds.

We lay there watching what Charlie called the mating ritual of young people.

The girls were making a big deal about stepping into the water, while the boys were trying to show how powerful they were, by swinging on the rope out into the middle of the pond, trying to mimic the sound Tarzan makes when he swings from tree to tree, or when he tries to get the attention of the little monkey that followed him around.

"Now don't that blow your dress up. It's a pure shame the way they are acting. If the girls had come out here all by themselves, you could just about bet your last dollar Sonny, well if you had a last dollar to bet that is, that the girls would not act so girlish or should I say so silly. They would have jumped straight into the water," Charlie said

"Take My Cousin, Sherry. She acts just like these girls, however she would not have a single bit of trouble pulling the heads off baby pigeons, but let some boy be within fifty yards of her, then watch, she would act like she was scared to death of baby pigeons. Giggling around and all, it's just makes me sick at my stomach watching her act the fool," Charlie said.

"Boy Charlie, all you need is a couch and you could become one of them doctors that cure people that are nuts," Bruce whispered.

We boys lay there for several minutes waiting for all four of them to get together. We thought it would be a lot funnier if we zapped them all at once.

Jay and Kerrie would stand together and talk just a little, then kiss. Jeffrey Hines was still in the middle of the matting game, making fun of Debra splashing water on her, pulling her arm. All the while she is giggling and keeps saying, "You better stop it are you'll be sorry."

After a few minutes of this, Jeffrey seemed to get up a little courage, because he walked up close to Debra and gave her a kiss. You could tell the mating ritual was in full bloom because both couples hugged and kissed.

Charlie whispered to us, "Okay," and he started to turn the small crank as fast as he could.

The electric charge hit the two couples just as all their lips came together. They started shaking and jerking around something pure Dee awful. It was about the funniest thing any of us had ever seen. When Charlie stopped cranking, the couples stopped shaking. They pulled back with their eyes as big as saucers.

We boys figured they would all scream and run for the bank as if their lives depended on it, however all they did was stand there and look at one another.

"Looks like there in shock," Bruce said, as all five of us giggled under our breath.

They stood that way for what seemed like several seconds before Jeffery said, "What was that?"

"Think there could be an underground electric line that is leaking?" Debra asked, not screaming, but talking in a not so normal voice. It was more like the voice of someone fixing to go into a pure panic.

When stunned fish started floating to the top of the water, the two girls started to whimper. The boys, you could tell, tried to stay calm, however we could see the fear in their eyes as the expressions on their faces started to turn to panic.

"Whatever it was we better get out here before it happens again," Jay said.

With that, they turned to head for shore. When they took another step, Charlie went to cranking again. The four of them went to jerking and shaking around like the kids you see now and then on that dance show on television.

Then, Charlie would stop cranking let them take another step or two. Then, he would crank some more.

This went on every time they took a step. It happened five or six times, at least. Jake finally whispered to Charlie, "Better let them go, or they will be glowing for a week."

"Good thing the Baptist preacher didn't see them jerking around and all," Gary said.

"Why is that?" I asked.

"You know they don't allow dancing in the Baptist Church. Preacher might have thought they were all dancing," he said, laughing.

The four young lovers reported the electric shocks to the sheriff's office, an Oklahoma Highway patrol officer, as well as anyone else that would listen to them.

A couple of men from the coop closed the swimming hole for a couple of days to investigate. Finding nothing wrong, they chocked it up to young people's imagination.

Jake got his revenge because everyone in town started making fun of all four of them whenever they saw one of them.

Both girls got grounded for a month when their parents found out, because it seems the girls told their folks they were going to the church to volunteer their help that day.

None of us boys ever let on about what we did. It was our secret, well ours and Mr. Burgers that is.

Chapter Fifteen

That next morning, we boys were sitting in the small park talking about nothing much, just talking, trying to figure what we should do that day. A few of us wanted to go fishing. A couple wanted to just hang out.

Bruce and Jake finely came up with the idea to go out to Tuna Boat Bob's and hunt for the treasure that Bell Star was supposed to have buried somewhere on his hundred acre farm. She was supposed to have robbed some bank or train somewhere in Oklahoma.

Tuna Boat Bob lived just south of town. He lived alone since his wife died of what people in town called, lockjaw.

None of us boys had one little bit of a clue as to what lockjaw was. Best we could figure, it was something that caused your jaw to lock up as tight as Dick's hat band. We figured with her jaw all locked up tight like that, she wasn't able to get any food down. She must have starved plum to death, we thought.

Jake wondered why they didn't take old Tuna Boat Bob's wife to the dentist in Chickasha and have him pull her front teeth out. That way, they could just heat up a can of chicken noodle soup and pour it down the lady.

Gary figured once lockjaw sets in good and proper, a person's ability to swallow had to be affected. Pouring chicken noodle soup into the mouth of someone with lockjaw would more than not drown them.

Wouldn't be so hard to explain to the sheriff about a person just wasting away from being unable to eat, but it would be an altogether different problem trying to explain to the law if you were to drown someone with a can of chicken noodle soup. We were sure the sheriff would frown on a soup drowning a considerable amount.

When they buried Bobs' wife, he was so upset with her wasting away like she did, that he just up and packed a few things, locked up the house and went down to Louisiana. He got himself a job on a tuna or shrimp boat, at least a boat of some kind. Nobody is sure if it was a shrimp boat, tuna boat or one of them boats that catch them crab-looking things.

Anyways, Bob worked on that boat for a couple of years. Said the only reason he quit that line of work was because one afternoon a storm came up about as quick as quick can be. Said the wind got to blowing something awful. The way he told it, the wind in Oklahoma blows something awful as well. Said onetime he saw a small bunch of chickens. When he looked away for about a second, maybe two seconds, then turned back around again, there wasn't one feather left on any of them chickens. All there was, was twenty-five or thirty naked chickens scurrying around, wondering what the heck happened. Good thing it was summer, or else every one of them chickens would have froze plum to death, with no feathers.

Said when that wind came up out there on the boat, it scared him near to death. In Oklahoma, a fellow has a chance to hide from the wind, tornadoes and such in a ditch, or in a culvert pipe, or in the cellar if your people happen to have one, but out there in the ocean, there isn't one place to hide. Sure, you can run down in the hole of the boat but when the ship sinks, there you are drowned. If you're in the hole in the boat, you're drowned in the boat's hole. If you're blown overboard, well, you drown all the same. Said he didn't want to die in no ocean and let the sharks and all the other little swimming creatures nibble on him until he was just a bunch of bones lying on the sandy bottom of the ocean.

Soon as boat docked, he packed up everything he had, walked down to the bus station and bought a one-way ticket back to Verden.

When he got back, Bob told the town folks of his adventures. They just naturally started calling him Tuna Boat Bob. It really didn't matter what they called him, however he did like Tuna Boat Boy better than Shrimp Boat Bob. Whatever it was he said, it didn't matter all that much as long as he was on dry land with a place to hide from the winds and tornadoes and such.

He said iffin you get blown to death in Oklahoma, someone or other would always find you and lay you to rest in the ground, right and proper, just like a dead guy was suppose to be laid to rest.

A few years after he got back, but a couple of years before we boys were born, a fellow showed up in Verden with a map he won in a card game. It was a map of Verden. Showed the small creek running through Bob's place with a spot marked

"Dig here." Since the map was so old, the creek had changed over the years, no one knew right where "here" was.

At the bottom of the map it was signed Bell Star, or at least someone had signed Bell Stars name. Since no one in town had ever seen Bell Stars signature, everyone took it as being her true signature.

There wasn't anything that said gold, or silver. There was just that mark that said "Dig here." Everyone that ever got to see that map knew it had to be gold she robbed off some stage or train and buried. By the time the word got around town, it was gold she robbed for sure, and there was just so much of it, she had to bury it.

They said, now days, it had to be worth millions, if not millions of millions.

Wasn't long before people from as far away as Wichita Falls, Texas to Dodge City, Kansas were out on Bob's land, looking under this brush pile, or under that tree. Several of them digging in the creek itself. Looked like the land run of eighty-nine, several people thought. Only no one was running anywhere. They were just milling around on Tuna Boat Bob's land, driving poor old Tuna Boat half nuts.

Bob tried to run them folks off several times. He went out there screaming and hollering, "Get the heck off my land. Get out of here. I mean every one of you," but them folks all had the gold fever. Nothing was about to budge any of them until they got over that fever.

Someone said a fellow named Tommy Factor was feeling under an old broken tree trunk. Said he thought he felt a rope. Thinking it had to be the rope Bell herself must have tied onto a strong box full of gold, he gave it a heck of a yank, pulling it out. You can imagine the surprised look he must have gotten on his face when out came a five foot long rattlesnake.

Not to even mention the look that rattlesnake must have had on its face being pulled out like it was from its home. Before Tommy could let go, that snake whipped around biting old Tommy right smack through his blue denim shirt in the middle of his belly, about three inches above his belly button.

Tommy went to screaming, as well as the men and women standing close enough to him to catch what just happened. If the people had feathers on their heads, it would have looked like a bunch of Indians doing some kind of a war dance, or we hope our crops grow better, dance.

One old woman passed smooth out, seeing that snake latched on to Tommy's belly like it was.

One farmer had sense enough to pick up an old piece of broken tree branch and beat the snake to death before it cold bite anyone else.

Dub Barnes made Tommy lay down. Then, with his pocket knife, he cut exes across each fang mark. Then he went to sucking out as much of that poison snake venom as he could.

They loaded old Tommy up in a wagon and took him to the hospital in Chickasha hoping to get him some treatment before he met his maker face to face that very same day.

When they got him to the emergency room to let old Dr. Hess check him out, the doctor said it looked to him like everything was going to be okay because of all the poison sucking that Dub did, and Tommy being a fellow that liked his beer like he did, having such a beer gut, any poison Dub didn't suck out, just naturally couldn't make it out of his big gut without diluting down to about nothing.

Bob had to end up calling in the sheriff before any of them folks finely got the idea he meant it. Thank goodness, he didn't have a problem with the five of us trying to find something of the gold from time to time.

We didn't go out there all that much, only a couple of time each summer. Sometimes, we would look all day with great hopes of leaving the place rich beyond our wildest dreams. The only things we ever found were a 1938 half dollar, a pocket knife with a broken blade, one old rusted up bent unopened can of pork in beans. Charlie wanted to open it up with the broken knife and eat it right then and there.

It took some explaining that there was a good chance if he ate just one of the beans in that can, he would be dead before we could get him any help.

One thing about Charlie, he had no problem not eating something that might just kill him, or at least he wouldn't eat something he was sure might kill him. I do believe if whatever it was only had a fifty-fifty chance of killing or making him sick, he would take his chances with that.

When we got to Tuna Boat Bob's that day, he was fit to be tied. Apparently, his ex-sister-in- law came down the day before, wanting him to sell his place and split the money with him.

The way old Bob put it, she told him since her sister's jaw locked up like it did and killed her, and since she was her only living blood relative, she thought she was entitled to half of everything Tuna Bob now owned, because she was sure if there had been a will, she would have been in it.

He was walking around on his porch when we got off our bikes in front of the house. I thought that something bad happened or that he might have been hit by a bad case of tuna boat flashback, thinking he was about to be drowned or even Alzheimer's must have set in on him. The way he was acting, he would walk to one end of the porch and scream, turn and walk to the other end and scream at the top of his lungs again.

When he seen us boys, he more or less settled down a little. He was still talking under his breath a little as we walked up on the porch.

Bruce thought he was cussing, but cussing low enough that us boys wouldn't hear him.

"What's wrong Bob?" I asked.

"It's my sister-in-law. That girl isn't fit to be called a human," he said.

He told us what she wanted Said there was no way in heck he would give that good for nothing one red cent. Said all she ever did, was try to get something for nothing.

Told us onetime before his wife's jaw locked up like it did, she came down and borrowed six hundred dollars to go to beauty school. Bob thought that was a right fine idea, because he always thought she was an ugly girl. Said some girls are kind of ugly. Some are ugly but with pretty eyes, or a pretty nose. Not his sister-in-law. She was just plain ugly. Had an ugly nose, her eyes were not completely crossed, but a little crossed, just crossed enough to make her one hundred percent ugly.

Told his wife to give her the money if it could improve her looks enough so as to find a husband and get her away from them. Then six hundred dollars was a mighty cheap sum.

Bob wasn't so keen on the idea when he found out it wasn't to make her look any better, but to train her how to make other women look better.

But loving his wife like he did, he went ahead and let her give her sister the money.

If Bob had any malice in his heart, he would have murdered that girl right on the spot when he found out she took his six hundred dollars, bought a few new clothes, took a Greyhound bus to Pensacola Florida in order to find a husband at one of the Navy bases there.

She told them she went to several places that Sailors are known to hang out at when they are off duty. Only one sailor came up to talk to her. All he wanted was to ask if she was with the carnival in town. If so, he wanted to know about how to join up, because he had a juggling act that he thought the carnival people might like.

That made her so mad, she took the money she had left and came back home, giving up on the idea of becoming a Navy wife.

It wasn't but a few weeks after, that his wife's jaw locked up on her causing her to waste away.

Said all the time she was wasting away, her sister never came by or even offered to help her. Now, she shows up wanting something she has no right to.

We explained to him, all he had to do was get a lawyer from Chickasha or Anadarko. They would put a stop to it for him.

"Now why didn't I think of that?" he said.

We figured the only reason he hadn't thought of a lawyer was because his mind was so clogged up with hate and homicide for his sister-in-law.

He told us guys, we could go down look to our hearts content for Bell Star's stash of gold.

We spent the rest of the day looking at places we had looked at a hundred times before. The fun was in the looking, the dreaming what we would do with all that money. There wasn't one of us that thought we would really find anything but what is a boy supposed to do in the summer other than go on adventures?

Chapter Sixteen

That next Monday, we thought we would walk out to Mr. Barton's house see how Miss Brandey was doing. What we really had in mind was to borrow her again to see if we could pull that fainting goat trick on someone one more time.

Last summer, it worked out like a charm, getting it to faint in front of the two church ladies. We didn't need money for the carnival this year because it really wasn't that big of a deal last year. What we did need was Miss Brandey to tease a few of the girls that pestered us.

Walking down the dirt road, we came across the same bull that Charlie tried the bull nut slapping on last year.

"There he is Charlie. Want another go at the nuts?" I asked, smiling at him.

"Just shut your smart mouth," he said, smiling back at me.

"They're hanging right there," I said, looking at the others

"My mother still hasn't let me live it down, ripping my jeans like I did," he answered.

I let the subject about the bull drop because the Barton place came into view.

Mr. Barton was in his garden picking squash. For the life of me, I can't figure why anyone in their right mind would ever plant squash. To me it was something to be avoided at just about all costs.

Rising up with a hand full of squash, Mr. Barton asked, "Well what brings you boys out this way? Got to raise more money?"

"No sir, not this summer. We have no plans to go to the carnival or the fair. Had all the fun we could stand last summer," I answered.

"How is Miss Brandey Doing?" Jake asked.

You would have thought someone had used the bathroom in his oatmeal, the look he gave us.

"Let me tell you boys something: I love that goat, but the critter has done gone and broke my heart," he said, sitting down on one of the railroad ties he used to place around his garden.

"Yes sir, Miss Brandey done snuck off some night and got herself in the momma way. I hate to say this about her, but she is a lousy goat. No telling who the daddy goat might be," he said, placing the squash he just picked in a neat little pile at his feet.

"I just hope she didn't take up with old lady Waterman's goat," he said.

"Now don't get me wrong, the Waterman's goat is a fine goat. Be proud to have it come live with Brandey and me. It's old Wanda that I can't abide. She has to be about one of the meanest women in the county, if not the meanest," he said.

"To tell the truth, mean doesn't describe her good enough. I'd kind of op for the word 'vicious' to be used in front of the word mean. She is plum vicious mean," he said, looking first to one, then the other of us.

"I kind of figure she must have been friends with my wife before she went to live with her sister. No telling what my old wife might have told her about me, but you can bet it wasn't anything you might hear at church being spoken regular," he said.

"Wouldn't surprise me in the least if she didn't bring her Billie goat over here sometime while I was gone and let him have at Miss Brandey. Would be just like her, the old bat," he said.

"Now that I think about it, I am sure that is just what she done, cause my wife showed up for no good reason at all. Wasn't time for me to give her any money. No, she just showed up out of the blue, asking me if I was ready for her to come home now that Brandey was going to have babies," he said, looking surprised

"Now how in God's name did that old bitty know my Brandey was going to have a litter of baby goats? I'll tell you how. Her and that Wanda Waterman got together and planned this. Yes, that is exactly what those two old girls did; they done went and schemed on me."

I could see a little anger building up in him.

"That's why my wife asked if I was ready to move poor Miss Brandey out into the barn, let her move back, yes sir them two schemed on me just as sure as red is red and yeller is yeller," he said.

"The only ways I would ever let her move back in that house would be if the good Lord struck me down and kill me dead with a heart attack, or any other thing that kill's a fellow out right, if that happen then I would hope no one would find my body for a few day, no several day so I can lay there dead and start rotting sticking up the place making it plum unfit to live in that would show my wife, no that would show them both," he said.

"Wow Mr. Barton we didn't mean to upset you." Bruce said looking down at him.

"Well their little schemed isn't going to work," he said.

"Nope I'm not about to let her move back in here," he said.

"And when Miss Brandey has her babies I will string them together just like stringing ducks and parade them in front of Wanda, I know for a fact it will eat her alive not being able to say her goat was the daddy and placing a claim on one or more of the babies," he answered looking up at Bruce smiling ear to ear.

"Now boys it says just a plain as day a body is not suppose to lie, but I'm fixing to tell you right here in front of you and the good Lord his very self that when I trot them babies by Wanda I'm fixing to lie to her as if my life depended on it, I will tell her that Miss Brandey had eight babies, some fellow from Okie City is fixing to come down bring me a check for five hundred dollars because of the number of babies Miss Brandey had, some kind of a state no world record. That my darn well kill old Wanda with envy, if not make her fess up to the no good her and my wife were up to," he said still smiling

"You boys want to see Miss. Brandey?" Mr. Barton asked

"She is out back by the barn, just follow me," he said as he started walking

Miss Brandey was standing beside and old bathtub filled with water, she looked just the same to me as she did last summer when we used her to pull the prank on the two church ladies.

"Can you boys see her stomach it's a bit larger than it should be, that right there tells you she is in the motherly way," he said

We boys kind of looked at one another because I am sure the others were thinking the same thing I was thinking, that she looked just about the same as she always looked.

We shook our heads yes to his question, more in self-defense, or should I say in order not to get him started up on another story, which didn't work at all, because he started up anyway.

He talked and talked about all the things he wanted to do to Wanda and his wife. He thought about letting his wife move back in just so he could have the joy seeing her face when he kicked her out.

All he wanted to do to Wanda was sneak down to her place some dark night and let every critter she had on the place go. Let her spend a few days trying to round them all up again, however that would never be enough to turn his Miss Brandey into a slutty goat, but at least he would have a little satisfaction watching her trying to find her animals.

We sat around for several minutes as he vented his anger toward everything and everybody. As soon as we got a chance, we said our goodbyes.

We had come in hopes of using his goat again just for fun, but as upset as Mr. Barton was, it didn't take much for us to decide against that.

Chapter Sixteen

There seemed to be a lot of strange people living in Verden. I asked my grandmother about that once. Her reply to me was, "Boy, Verden, as small as it is, is purely plum-full of strange birds, and we have lots and lots of no-accounts living around here as well, however out little town is no different than any other town. Far as I know, every town has their number of no-accounts and strange acting people. No, Verden is about as good as a town as a fellow could ask for," she said.

I had to agree with her. To me, Verden had to be the best place in Oklahoma to grow up in.

Sure, we had some very strange people living here. I believe a couple of the strangest was Mr. and Mrs. Posey. They lived west of town about half of a mile. They were in the carrier pigeon business.

About any night you could find Mr. Posey somewhere around the old grain elevator trying to catch pigeons. They turned their carport into a pigeon coup, putting chicken wire all around it with a small door in the front.

The Posey's would keep the pigeons in the carport, feeding them all sorts of things. When they thought they had been in the cage long enough, Mr. Posey would load several of them in his old Dodge pickup, drive several miles away and let them go in hopes they would fly back home to the good life.

Mrs. Posey would wait for the bird's return, which never happened. In all the ten years, not a one of them ever came back to the carport.

We, along with several other people from town, thought that was what caused the couple to act the way they did. They couldn't seem to get along with anyone. When boys or girls happened to walk by their place, heading to either one of their friends house or just riding their bikes by, either Mr. or Mrs. Posey would come running out of the house screaming, "You kids better get out of here. You know you don't belong here. Now, scat!"

It got so everyone wanted to bypass their house all together, so they didn't have to put up with the Posey's screaming at them. It meant they had to go a couple of miles out of the way, but to some, it was well worth it.

We boys had forgotten about the Posey's one afternoon walking to the woods to play cowboys and Indians. Really, it was who could outfox the others. Okay, it was a thirteen year-old boy's version of hide and seek.

Just as we got in front of the Posey's house, Mr. Posey jumped up from behind some scrubs, and Mrs. Posey jumped out of the tall grass across the road from us.

"What the heck are you boys doing out here?" Mr. Posey screamed, so loud I'm sure they must have heard it on Main Street.

"You Brats," screamed Mrs. Posey in unison with her husband.

You could tell which of us boys used the restroom before coming out here, because I near wet myself. Jakes said he spilled some water from the canteen he was carrying. That seemed strange to me, since the lid looked to be still screwed on. I didn't say anything or ask him how he spilled it with the lid still on, because I'm sure I would have wet myself if I had not gone an hour before.

Bruce took off running, not looking back for several yards.

Charlie let out a little girl scream.

When we all got our wits back, we took off running, just like Bruce.

Up the road about a quarter of a mile Charlie asked, "Good Gosh almighty what in the world is wrongs with them people? Are they nuts?"

We all started to laugh once we realized we were not about to be beat plum to death by an old man and woman.

We knew just as well as every kid in Verden knew what would happen walking near the Posey house. We just dropped our guard this time. You can bet we didn't plan to do that again.

"Are we going to let him and that old bitty get away with that?" Jake asked.

"What can we do? They are grownups. Not much you can do to a grownup without getting a whooping when someone finds out about it," Bruce said.

When we returned to town, we took the Posey detour, or what people started to call it because of those two old nuts. It was not so much because we were afraid of the two of them either. We just didn't want to take a chance of getting the pee scared out of us again.

We all sat around on the depot steps, talking about what we could do to get even with them.

We came up with the idea to try and scare the crap out of Mr. Posey. Now that we had that idea, we had to figure out just how to go about doing it.

It was almost impossible to do anything to scare him on his own property. With that figured out, we decided to do it when he was trying to catch pigeons some night at the grain elevator.

Remembering how we got the train engineer, we decided to try the same thing on Mr. Posey.

The next day, we all met at Bruce's house, because his sister had all the makings it took to build a large paper Mache pigeon. We thought if anything could scare Mr. Posey it would have to be a pigeon about the size of a fifty-five gallon barrel or bigger.

We worked on that pigeon for several hours. What we ended up with after we finished didn't really look all that much like a pigeon. To me, it looked more like a big volcano with wings. We believed the reasoning behind that, was that we let Bruce's little sister help build the thing. All she had ever built was a paper Mache volcano. That's why our pigeon resembled one of those, rather than a pigeon.

That next night, in order to be out after dark, each one of us made some kind of an excuse to our parents.

I told my mother that several of us kids were going to meet at the church to do some praying for things in general, like world peace, a cure for cancer and maybe even lock-jaw.

It had always been my thought that telling an outright lie could send you straight to hell, but if you told an outright lie with a little truth mixed in with it, you might just have a chance to square that with God. At least, it was a chance once you were standing up in front of Him, Him looking down on you the way I was told He would be.

That's why I asked all the guys to meet up at the church. When we were all together, I said to them, "Gosh, I pray everything goes good."

After I said that, I was covered completely. I did go to church, and I did pray, so I was square with my mother and that squared me up as well with the Lord himself.

We boys made our way to the grain elevator in the dim moonlight. As we pushed the large steel door open, it made a high pitched sound like when someone drags their nails down a blackboard, only with a little deeper pitch to it.

When we stepped inside, what little moonlight we had disappeared inside the grain elevator. I thought that Charlie and Gary would never be able toget that paper pigeon inside. I thought at first, we were going to have to de-wing the thing to get it through the door.

Jake had been here a couple of times before, so he knew where the office was. When he turned the office light on, it lit up the elevator room up just enough so we wouldn't bump into this or that.

I couldn't afford to go home with torn jeans or a bloody knee because that would be a dead giveaway that we had been up to no good, because a kid doesn't get their clothes torn or cut up praying.

Gary climbed up into the rafters as high as he could, then dropped a rope down to us to tie the volcano-looking pigeon onto. The thing was a little too heavy for him to pull up by himself, so I climbed up to help him pull the darn thing up.

On my way up, I had to scare pigeons off their roost to get up where Charlie was waiting. Once they were scared off their roost, they would fly around a bit in the dark, confused until they found another place to roost for the night.

When we finely got it up, we laid it backward with a rope attached to it. That way, when we wanted it to pop up, all we had to do was pull on the rope.

We finished up just in time because light appeared though the window. We hoped it was Mr. Posey and not the sheriff, because there would be no explaining that to our folks when they came to Chickasha to get us out of county jail.

Jake ran to the office to shut the light off. The rest of us hid behind what we though must be large bales of cotton.

We heard the squeal of the iron door just as we saw the light from a powerful flashlight.

Bruce whispered to me, "A person must need a lot of light to blind the pigeons in order to make it easier to catch them."

Every one of us let out the breath we had been holding in hoping it wasn't the sheriff coming to arrest us, when we saw Mr. Posey in the light of his flashlight.

He was caring the flashlight in one hand and a brown gunny sack in the other, while trying to make the sound that pigeons make, a little hoot-hoot every few seconds. We figured he thought hoot-hooting like that would make the pigeons trust him as one of their own.

When he started climbing up the ladder to grab a pigeon before placing it in the gunny sack, we did everything possible to not start laughing out loud at him and his hoot-hooting.

Charlie actually bit his own arm, bringing a small amount of blood, to keep from laughing out loud and giving us away.

When Mr. Posey was less than five feet away from where we placed the volcano-pigeon, Bruce and Jake gave the rope a good hard jerk. Up popped the paper Mache pigeon. When his flashlight shown on the Mache-pigeon for just a second, Mr. Posey gave one last hoot-hoot under his breath, then he dropped the flashlight altogether. Next, he let go of the gunny sack. Then he let go of the piece of steel he was holding onto. As he was falling, I thought I heard a hoot-hoot followed by a blood-curdling scream. When he hit the bottom, we heard the wind rush out of him.

Jumping up and trying to suck in enough air to scream, he didn't try to retrieve his flashlight or the gunny sack. He grabbed hold of the door handle, letting out the most pitiful scream I have ever heard. In what light there was, he limped and tried to run back to his pickup. Not even taking the time to turn the pickup lights on, he started backing up. He backed all the way down the street, not bothering to turn around or turn his lights on.

We boys heard later on that Mr. and Mrs. Posey had gone out of the homing pigeon business altogether. They bought a few goats and a couple of cows and became farmers. We never did find out if they still tried to scare the pee out of kids that walked by their house.

Chapter Seventeen

My grandmother asked me to go over to Rosa Nunnelley's house to help her with a few chores that she needed done, and she better not hear I took any pay from the old woman. If Rosa wanted to make me a sandwich that would be fine; other than, that nothing else was acceptable.

Rosa was an old lady that lived a couple blocks west of the old jail. She was as nice as anyone in Verden. She was the type that would do just about anything for you. That is why people tried to help her a lot, now that she was so old that she had a hard time doing for herself.

When I got there, she had me hoe the weeds out of her garden, pick up a few limbs that had blown in her yard from the thunder storm we had a few days back, and fix a small spot in the chicken wire fence she had around her house that she said she used to keep unwanted critters out.

At noon, she called me in to have lunch with her. As we sat there talking, I noticed a coffin in the other room sitting on the bed. The mattress had been removed to accommodate the coffin.

As I sat there eating my chicken sandwich, I wanted to ask her about the coffin something awful, however I had no idea if it was polite to ask someone about a coffin in their bedroom.

If it had been a doll, or a baseball, or something normal that people keep as keepsakes, I would have had no problem asking about those items, but a coffin was a different matter altogether because if someone happened to be inside of it, that might cause an even bigger problem.

She must have understood I had questions because of the way I kept looking into the room containing the coffin. She had seen me turn my head several times to look into what I later named "the coffin room."

"It's a coffin," she said, looking at me.

"Ho," is all I could answer because my mouth was half-full of sandwich.

"Well, as much as expensive as things are getting these days, bread is up to twenty cents a loaf. I don't use the stuff, but gas I'm told, is near twenty-five cents a gallon. Can you believe twenty-five cents a gallon? They must think the stuff is made out of pure gold," she said, placing her hand up to her face.

"And boy, did you know I sent a letter to my sister in Kansas. I hate to say it, but that stamp cost me four cents. I felt like I was being robbed just the same as if that postman was holding a gun on me. Four cents! I hope them people in Washington are happy making things so expensive that a common person can't afford to buy themselves nothing to make life a little better.

"That's why I have that coffin in there. I picked it up from a fellow who thought his father needed one, only to find out there was nothing wrong with his father other than pure Dee laziness. His father was not sick the least little bit, so I got it for hundred and twenty dollars. That was just after the war. Wouldn't surprise me one little bit if you was to buy a coffin these days, one would cost near five hundred dollars. Heck, I'm not about to pay five hundred dollars for some box that no one will ever see but the one time," she said to me, smiling.

"I wouldn't want this to get around to people in town, but I sleep in that thing at night. I figure once the good Lord calls me to his glory and I get sent home in that box, I will have a darn good idea what it feels like to be in it. Besides, how many people do you know that has ever gotten out of one," she said, laughing out-loud and slapping the table, turning the ketchup and salt over.

As I was working on the fence, I got to laughing about what Rosa said about the coffin. I figured there had to be a way I could use this to my advantage.

Finishing up with the fence, I knocked on her door to tell her I was leaving. When she answered it, she had a new crisp dollar bill in her hand. "Here, take this boy. I know it's not much, but it's something for helping me," she said.

I would kind of liked to have taken that dollar, buy some candy and one of those ice cream push-up for me and the guys, but between not getting a push-up or not getting a couple flyswatter licks across the naked butt, I said, "No, Mrs. Nunnelley, I can't take your money. I was glad to help out."

"Well boy, it just don't seem right to make you work most the day and not give you a little something in return," she answered.

"I'll tell you what Mrs. Nunnelley, I won't take the money but there is something you can do for me, if you would." I said.

"Well, if I can. I don't get out much you know. Come in tell me what it is you want," she said, holding the door open.

I told her about what Mr. Finchmoore and I did to the guy last summer. I thought if she would help me, I might be able to pull something off again on my buddies. She agreed to help.

We had it arranged that I would show up at her window just after dark the next night. She agreed to have her curtains open so we boys would be able to look inside.

The next day, I asked the guys if they would like to share a watermelon at my house that night. Of course, they all agreed they would love that. I knew they would, because who doesn't like watermelon.

I told them I had to go shut off the water sprinkler at Mrs. Nunnelley's house around dark to keep from flooding her garden. The guys all agreed to go with me - one for all; all for one.

That evening, a few minutes before dark, we headed to Mrs. Nunnelley's house to shut off the water. The conversation was on about everything thirteen year-old boys find to talk about.

Walking in front of the movie house, I started telling them about helping Rosa with different tasks around her house. I told them just how strange she seemed to me. Said she wouldn't let me come in her house. She would only come out in the daylight. I told them when she asked me to come over and shut the water off at night, she wore large sunglasses, which seemed strange because she would never come out of the shadows.

"Wow, she must not like being around people," Jake said.

"Sounds like a vampire," Bruce said.

"Bela Lugosi acted just like that in the movie, 'Dracula.' You guys remember that?" he asked, kind of excited.

"Sure I remember. Scared the crap out of me," I said

" Bela Lugosi is a great actor. 'I want to bite your neck and suck your blood,'" Gary said, trying to talk like the famous actor.

When we reached the house, I walked up to the side of the house just under her window, reached into the brush as if I was turning a valve shutting the water off. Mrs. Nunnelley was true to her word. The curtains were completely drawn. There were five or six candles burning, giving off just enough light so as to be able to see everything in the room. The coffin was lit up a lot better than I hoped. It had kind of an eerie look to it in the dim candle light.

Looking out toward the guys, I motioned for them to come up. The four of them walked up next to me, also looking into the window.

"Great! Now we are becoming Peeping Toms, peeping in on a old woman old enough to be my grandmothers mother. No, we couldn't peek in on Mary Sue Bailey who is someone young and good-looking. No, we have to peep in on an old wrinkled up old woman," Jake said, looking in the window.

I believed all four of them recognized the coffin at the same time.

"What the crap? What the crap?" someone said. I don't know which one it was that said it. I was too busy doing my best not to laugh and give it all away.

"What the heck! Why does that old woman have a coffin in her house?" Charlie asked.

"Who's to know? I bet she didn't have the money to bury her husband when he passed away. Must have run out of money once she bought the coffin," Bruce said.

"Now, you know that's not it. There's laws that make you bury people within a day or two after they die," I said, trying to juice the guys up some more.

For several seconds, the guys stood mesmerized by the coffin and the candles burning in the room.

"This is kind of creepy. Think she is nuts?" Jake asked.

"A lot nuts if you ask me," Bruce answered to no one in particular.

"Hush! Look!" Charlie said in a whisper.

Right on cue, the coffin lid started to open very, very slowly. The guys standing around me became as quiet as what my grandmother called a church mouse.

The first thing that appeared was a small wrinkled hand appeared when the lid opened. Then, together we saw Mrs. Nunnelley slowly sit up. She slowly turned her head to face the window. It was so scary, it even scared me and I was a party to what was happening.

"Think she can see us?" I asked, turning to look at the others. To my surprise, Charlie was the only one left standing there. You could see he was visibility shaken.

"Let's get the heck out of here," he said

"Look!" I said

Mrs. Nunnelley was stepping out of the coffin when he looked back into the window.

"Holy crap! Holy crap!" Charlie said as he turned to run.

Charlie was as white as a sheet when he took off.

I had no clue Charlie was as fast as he was. Looked to me as if he crossed the street going toward the back of his house in two steps. I knew I would never catch him. I was smart enough to know you could never catch a thirteen year-old boy when a vampire just scared the crap out of him.

Charlie would have knocked a hole in the door if it had been closed. When I got there, I was kind of scared to tell him it was all a set-up.

I got him a glass of water to help him kind of calm down. The way he was shaking, I thought it might take a couple of days and several glasses of water to do the trick.

He was mad when he found out that Mrs. Nunnelley wasn't a vampire about to suck the blood out of half the people living in Verden.

The other guys also took it kind of hard, but then once the fear passed, they also got a kick out of what Rosa and I did.

Three days after our vampire experience, Mrs. Nunnelley got to use her hundred and twenty dollar coffin for real.

My grandmother told me over biscuits and gravy one morning a few days after the vampire prank, that Mrs. Nunnelley passed on to be with her sister in glory land.

Being thirteen, I had a hard time trying to figure out why people wanted to call it glory land, Heaven or any such thing as that. To me, it didn't seem like much of a place when all you had was a bunch of dead people sitting around talking about what they did or didn't do while they were down on un-glory land.

There wouldn't be no baseball, basketball, nor would you be able to play pranks on one another. I was sure that would irritate God, pulling pranks in glory land. I wasn't all that into girls yet, sure I really liked Mary Sue Bailey, and with any luck at all, one day I had plans to look her square in the eyes and say, "Mary Sue Bailey, I sure like the fire out of you."

That just would not happen today, and not tomorrow, maybe not even for a few years. Sure, I had guts to do things. Just didn't have the guts quite yet to say such a thing to her.

I asked my grandmother what happened to Mrs. Nunnelley, hoping I hadn't caused her demise by asking her to be part of my prank on the guys.

If it had been because I involved her in the prank, I wondered if I was looking at being stalked by the sheriff again. Seemed to me, a lot of things I was involved in made the word "sheriff" come up a lot.

It came as a big relief to me when she told me Mrs. Nunnelley pasted on to glory land because her heart just gave out when she was at the post office, mailing a letter.

I know my grandmother must have thought I was a strange kid, or a kid with no feeling when I kind of smiled and laughed to myself, because she gave me a weird look I had never seen before. If only she knew about what Mrs. Nunnelley told me about the four-cent stamp, she would have smiled as well, I bet.

Chapter Eighteen

One afternoon, Jake and I were sitting on the little bench in front of the pool hall, waiting on the other guys to show up. We had no idea what we were all going to do that day, however when you're thirteen, the world has many an option. All you have to do is use your mind to bring your imagination into focus.

I was talking to Jake about what it would be like going into the eighth grade. I wondered what he thought our teachers and the other kids would be like. Then I saw Mary Sue Bailey walking our way with a girl named Loretta Guin.

I really liked Mary Sue, however Loretta was another story altogether. Loretta had been my lab partner in biology class. She disliked boys back then as much as we boys disliked girls.

Loretta, I have to admit, was good at showing she didn't like boys. While dissecting a frog one afternoon, Loretta and I had this little dead frog pinned on its back, each leg stretched out with a pin to hold it in place.

Six or seven extra pins had been provided to each couple, so as you went about dissecting the frog, we could pin each thing back as it was explained by Mr. Lapatch, our biology teacher.

I was looking around at some of my friends making stupid faces like boys do. Loretta took that opportunity to stick several of the extra pins in the private parts of the frog, or what I was sure were the private part area of that dead frog. I didn't really know anything about a frog's private parts area however.

As Mr. Lapatch walked around the room explaining how this organ in the frog worked compared to a human, he walked up to Loretta and my frog. Seeing the needles poked into the frog's private area, his face became red. I figured Loretta would be getting a good scolding. Heck, if I were lucky, she would get a trip to the principal's office.

Mr. Lapatch didn't even look at Loretta. He looked directly into my eyes and before I could say, "Woo, wait a minute Mr. Lapatch! I didn't have anything to do with that little stunt. It was all Loretta."

Loretta said, "Mr. Lapatch, it's so hard to be a lab partner with a boy when they won't take these projects serious," in a please-help-me voice.

Mr. Lapatch took hold of my arm said, "Sonny, you have a smutty, smutty, smutty mind."

Mr. Lapatch was famous for using the word smutty when dressing down someone. Carl Larson was the only boy to ever get the word smutty used twice in the same sentence. He held the record for the number of times smutty was used on him, and that was because he came into the classroom with his arm on a girls shoulder just before class started.

Now it looked like I was the new record-holder, having had it used on me three times in the same sentence, a record that would go down in infamy, to quote Mr. Roosevelt's WWII speech.

All I could think was, "Look out flyswatter. Here I come," as soon as the word "smutty" reached my grandmother.

I wanted to call Loretta a bold-face liar for blaming me, but I would have been shunned for the rest of my school years, if not my life. I might have to even move out of Verden altogether for tattling on a girl, something that just wasn't done.

I was sent to the office along with the dead frog. Walking toward the Principles office, I was sure there would soon be no difference between me and that stupid dead frog I was carrying with the extra pins in its private area.

The principal went easy on me. Instead of giving me licks, I had to stay after school and sit in his office for an hour each day for a week.

When my Grandmother found out what happened, I was sure she was about to beat me to death with her stupid flyswatter, however when I explained to her what happened, she believed me. For that, I felt very lucky and yes, thankful.

When the two girls came up next to us they stopped. Loretta asked if I had cut up any frogs lately. I sure wished she was a boy about then.

Mary Sue looked me in the eyes and asked, "Sonny I was just wondering if you might like to come to my house for supper tonight."

Talking about putting a guy in a bind, Mary Sue did just that to me, asking me to dinner at her house in front of one of my best friends.

I could think of nothing I would rather do then eat supper with her, but why couldn't she have asked me when we were alone? I knew that would have been near impossible, because I never seemed to be alone. One or more of the guys were always with me.

If there had been a slim chance of me being alone, Mary Sue still had the devil girl with her. If I said yes, everyone in Verden, probably part of Chickasha and Anadarko would also know, as big a mouth as Loretta had.

I wanted to say yes right off the bat, but Jake was taking in every word and action without blinking an eye. This was all he needed to tease me for the rest of my life.

"You're asking me on a date?" I asked her, trying to save face however not sure if asking that was in anyway saving face.

I will say this for Mary Sue, she saw the predicament I was in with Jake and devil-girl both watching.

"Good gosh no. I wouldn't date you if you were the last boy on earth," she said.

Wow, I could have reached over and planted a big kiss right square on Mary's mouth for saying that, getting me out of such a predicament with my friend.

"Why then are you asking?"

"It's my dad. He needs someone to talk to other than my mother and my sister and me about men things. I thought it would be nice to have you come meet him and talk to him about different things," she answered.

I made a mental note if I was ever alone with her, I would thank her and if she didn't seem to care, I would plant that kiss right smack on her.

That seems to satisfy both Jake and the devil-girl. I could tell by the looks they both had.

So, I answered her with the best non-excited voice I could muster up. "Sure. What time?"

"We sit down to eat around five-thirty. Why don't you get there, say around five. That way you and my dad can talk," she answered.

I took my first boy-meets-girl shower. That type of shower lasts a lot longer than a regular because a regular just gets the dirt off. In a boy meets girl shower, you use at least a whole bar of soap, unless it's the lye soap my grandmother makes. With lye soap, you can get several showers with one bar, and while you're at it, take several layers of skin at the same time.

If you really take a good boy-meets-girl shower, if you're lucky enough to have started growing hair under your arms, you wash there so much that all that is soon gone. When you step out, you're as wrinkled as poor old Mrs. Nunnelley was the last time they put her in her coffin.

I was going to wear my funeral clothes, but my Mother put the nix to that. Said there was a better than good chance I would come home with either the pants ripped open or something spilled on the jacket.

I just wore my newest jeans and a clean OU t-shirt. I figured if one of the guys happened to see me walking to Mary Sue's house, they wouldn't think anything strange about my dress.

I arrived about fifteen minutes before five. I knew how long it took to get to her house, but there was always a chance I could get held up by a train, or a storm. There were thousands of things that could have stopped me from getting there on time. That's why I opted to leave fifteen minutes early.

I waited beside Mary Sue's house in the scrubs until I heard the big clock on the bank start striking five. I didn't want to knock on the door one minute early or one minute late. I just wasn't sure how this dinner thing was support to work.

As I knocked on the door ,I remembered something I had forgotten completely.

A year before I was knocking on this same door with my friends telling Mr. Bailey we didn't know for sure who's baby Mary Sue was carrying. We just about got killed over that little deal.

As the door opened, my legs started to shake, because I thought that maybe Mary Sue was setting me up and getting even for what we did to her last year. Was this going to be my last day on earth? Was her father going to get me into the house and then beat me to death with a blunt object, like a hammer, or a shovel? Or was Mrs. Bailey going to shake some kind of poison in the mashed potatoes they served me, or on the chicken fried steak that I could smell cooking. I prayed if I got poisoned to please not let them put it on a chicken fried steak as that was my favorite food of all time. I would hate to go to glory land with a piece of chicken fried steak stuck in my throat with poison on it.

It's hard to smile when you're about to have homicide done to you.

When Mr. Bailey came to the door, he just looked down at me for several seconds before he finely asked me in.

Once inside, even as nervous as I was, things seemed pleasant. Mr. Bailey even smiled at me several times. I figured he either forgot I was one of the boys that made him lose his religion last summer, or he decided to forgive me for it, either for Mary's sake, or he didn't want to mess up his trip to glory land when his time came to take that trip.

I sat on the couch at one end while Mary sit on the other end, getting up from time to time to help her mother in the kitchen.

The way things were going, I figured it was poison they would be using on me. That left no outright wounds that the cops would pick up on.

When we sat down to eat, I sat next to Mr. Bailey. I figured it was so he could get the most pleasure out of watching the poison take effect on me and have a close up view of me rolling around on the floor, kicking around down there, gasping for air at his feet.

Just before we started to eat, Mr. Bailey said a little prayer. He said his out loud. I said mine to myself and God under my breath. "God if these people are fixing to kill me, I am sure sorry for all the trouble I have caused you these last thirteen years. I would be proud to meet up with you in glory land if you see fit."

I watched real close to what was served me. If one of the family took something like potatoes or gravy or green beans, then I would take some. If not, you can bet I didn't either. If they had plans to murder me, I wasn't going to make it easy for them.

After supper, Mrs. Bailey asked if I would like some strawberry shortcake. I loved strawberry shortcake, however I knew then that was it. Strawberry shortcake comes in individual servings, individual servings made in the kitchen out of sight. Yes, that was how they were going to do me in. "No thank you Mrs. Bailey. I couldn't eat another thing," I said.

The truth was, I was just about to pull a Charlie, eat the shortcake and take my chances. Instead, I just sat and watched all the others enjoy theirs.

After we ate, I sat around talked with Mary and her family for a couple of hours. To my surprise, everything went great. Not Mary or anyone else in her family tried to beat me to death with anything that was blunt. As far as I felt, I felt pretty darn good. They either used a very slow acting poison on me, or no poison at all.

Around seven-thirty, I decided I best get home. Sure didn't want to wear out my welcome. Mary walked me out onto the front porch to say goodbye. I just about was ready to kiss her. The only problem I had with that was, I didn't have the first clue how to go about it.

Was I support to ask if I could kiss her, or should I just grab a hold of her and get it done like Clark Gable did Doris Day in the movie Teacher's Pet? We boys went to see that one only because there wasn't a Johnny Mack Brown cowboy picture showing.

Or, was I support to just pucker up and lean into it, like a fellow would lean into a pitcher's fast ball while playing baseball.

What if I puckered up, leaned into it, and she pulled away. I would look as dumb as dumb could look, all puckered up with only air to kiss.

I thought what the heck, just as I was puckering up, her dad opened the door said, "Better come on in now Mary."

I felt kind of a relief, not that I didn't want to kiss her, but I just didn't want to look the fool doing it.

Mary did as her father said. She turned and said goodbye to me and walked back into the house as her father held open the door.

Stepping completely out of the house, letting the screen door close behind him, he said to me, "You be careful walking home Sonny. All kinds of things go bump in the night. Might even be some father of a young girl that you did or said something about, out in the darkness just waiting for you." He was smiling like he knew something I didn't know.

"You know what I'm talking about, don't you?" he asked

I knew just what he was talking about. If I had any thoughts he had gotten over what we did last year, I knew right then and there he hadn't.

I hated that walk home. I was afraid around every corner that he was waiting for me. A cat jumped out from a trash can next to the pool hall. That cat almost scared me to death. I had a hard time sleeping that night and several nights following, because every time I closed my eyes I saw Mr. Bailey walking up on me, carrying a large bowl of strawberry shortcake.

Chapter Nineteen

We boy's had become really good friends with Mr. Finchmoore over the last several months. He seemed to always be there if we needed to ask him a question about someone in town. All the years he lived in Verden, he had come to know a little about everyone in town.

If we needed him to help with a prank or something, he was always willing to help. That's why we boys decided to pull a prank on him.

We decided since he was always making trips to the mailbox to give the town's people something to talk about, why not put something in the box for him to find.

Charlie wanted to put a draft notice in, but where would we find the right type of paper to look official enough to fool him? Besides, he would know it was a joke because men around eighty years old didn't normally get draft notices.

Bruce said we should put a note in the box from his ex-wife's lover, telling him she wanted to come home. We decided we better not do that because it could cause him to go into a

183

heart attack. When the sheriff found the note, well there we would go again.

Jake said let's put a sack of poop in to see what he thinks about that. Again, we decided against that, even it if was a darn good idea. We just thought more of him than to let him reach in his mail box pull out a sack full of poop. What if it broke open? That would mess his hands up; no telling what it would do to the inside of the mailbox.

What we did come up with was a love note. We decided Mr. Finchmoore needed a secret admirer. I liked this idea best because not one of us boys could spell worth a darn, and we couldn't write nice enough to look like a woman's writing. So, to make it look authentic, I would ask Mary Sue to join in on the prank. That way, the note would look good. I would get to be around Mary Sue without the guys thinking anything about it. For me it was a win, win situation.

The first note that we put in his mailbox said, "Dear: Mr. Finchmoore, I hope you don't think me too presumptuous or too forward, but I saw you at the drug store a couple of days ago picking up some Q-tips and a few other things and I just wanted you to know that I think you're sure a fine looking older feller."

Mary Sue put the word presumptuous in the note because we had no clue what it meant. We just took her word that it made the note sound more like it came from a grown-up.

When Mr. Finchmoore left for town, Jake ran over to the mailbox and stuck it in.

Then we went across the tracks to the depot to wait and watch for him to return.

When he came back from town, the first thing he did as always, was check the mail. We couldn't see the expression on his face very good from the depot. What we could see of it, it looked like he picked up a bag of poop, the way he shook it turned it this way and that looking at it.

He sat his small bag of groceries down next to his feet, opened the letter, then looked around like he was about to break the law. Then, blowing the letter open he took out the note inside, looked around again making sure he was alone and then he opened the note and read it.

Stuffing the note and envelope into his pocket, he again looked around. Seeing no one, he picked up his things and walked up to his house and went inside.

The next note I took over around midnight. I had to watch what I was doing because Mr. Finchmoore had a habit of checking his mail at odd hours, day or night. If he caught me, the prank would be over.

The note I took over said, "Dear Mr. Finchmoore, You are driving me nuts the way you walk out to your mail box, then the way you strut going back to your house. I have a very difficult time sleeping at night thinking of you and your bottom as you strut around."

Mr. Finchmoore never mentioned the notes to me or the others, but I could feel him looking through us, trying to get something out of us to see if we might be involved with this secret admirer thing that was going on with him.

The next note that was delivered by Bruce said, "Fiche, I believe I'm in love with you. As I hide in these weeds, watching you, my true love, my heart is racing. It feels like it is about to burst out of my tiny chest. Please, Fiche, wear that red shirt of yours that shows the gray hair on your chest. Oh, the gray hairs on your chest! What I wouldn't give to run my fingers through them."

I believe that one got to him, because when Jake and I were sitting on his porch with him he asks us if either of us had noticed anyone messing around his house or mailbox.

We explained to him that we hadn't seen anyone around, however we also explained that we weren't around much.

"Well boys, seems I got me a nut case stalking me. I have been getting all kinds of love notes in the mail. At first I thought it was one of you boys joking with me. But now I believe it's got to be some crazy person," he said

Took everything Bruce and I had in us to keep a straight face.

"Think you should call the law?" I asked in the most sincere voice I could come up with.

"No, I'm sure whoever it is will lose interest soon enough," he said

The next note I delivered myself while he was walking back to the house from checking the mail. I acted like I was going somewhere. Then when he turned to head back to his house, I slipped it in. I thought he was turning around about to catch me, but he didn't.

The note said, "My Dearest Finche, I know that the moon and sun must come up to give me the light to see the face of my beloved, your face. I pray that you will leave your window open again so I can watch you sleep, my love. Your snoring to me is like the sweet sound of a nightingale. I wanted to crawl in your window embrace you, my sweet."

When I went over the next day you could see he was visibly shaken. He was biting his finger nails, pacing from one end of his porch to the other. When he stopped pacing, he would sit down either on one of the chairs on the porch or on the edge of the porch itself. He wouldn't sit there but for a couple of seconds, then he was up pacing again.

I kind of felt sorry for him. I wondered if I should tell him it was us boys. I sure didn't want to cause him to have a stroke over our little joke. I decided I would talk to the guys and tell them it was time to let him in on the joke before he stroked out.

Mr. Darby, the old man that seemed to always be playing dominos with the other old men at the pool hall, had a stroke. I was told by Mr. Orr, he was playing one minute, the very next minute he tossed the two dominos he was holding straight up in the air, then he sat straight up in the chair, getting as stiff as one of those manikins you see over in the Sears and Roebucks store in Chickasha.

Apparently, he spent several days in the hospital, then several months trying to learn to walk and talk again. He never was able to use the left side of his body very well after that stroke.

I sure didn't want to be the cause of Mr. Finchmoore having a stroke, so no matter what the others said tomorrow, I would tell him the truth.

We guys talked it over the next day and decided to go ahead and tell him it was us all the time and that he didn't have a secret admirer.

We boys got to his house around noon. I called him outside, telling him we wanted to tell him something.

I, like the rest of us, hoped he would take the joke or prank in good spirits and not be mad and kick us off his porch and out of his life.

We asked him to sit down. Then I started telling him what we had done, that we were his secret admirer, We hated tricking him, but we meant it all in good fun, same as the joke he helped me play on the others last summer.

"How can that be?" he asked, looking concerned.

"You boys have to be mistaken, because I have her in the house as we speak. We are talking marriage because when we met, we knew it was love at first sight," he said.

I looked at the other guys while they all looked from one to the other and then back at me in total confusion. I was worried that we had gone too far with the joke and drove Mr. Finchmoore completely nuts.

"Honey, hurry back," came a female voice from inside the house.

Mr. Finchmoore looked at us, winked and made a gesture like he was hot.

"Isn't love just about the sweetest thing going?" he asked us.

It's a good thing there weren't many flies around, the way all our jaws were hanging open.

"Honey, why don't you come out and meet the boys. You might even know one or two of them," he hollered through the screen door.

When the door opened, I thought I would pass plum out. If the others jaws could have open wider, I am sure they would have when my grandmother walked out on the porch.

I wanted to scream and run for any cover available that was close enough to hide my embarrassment and the shame I was feeling. My joke had turned into my worst nightmare.

I kind of felt relief when my grandmother pulled her famous flyswatter from behind her back and went to swatting every boy in site. She was swinging so fast and hard, she even hit Mr. Finchmoore a couple of times. That didn't seem to matter to him much, him being bent over laughing as he was.

"I should beat the skin plum off every one of you little no-accounts. Do you have nothing better to do than pester Mr. Finchmoore with all your sex talk?" she said as she connected a couple hits on Jake, one on Charlie.

"It's a darn good thing he is smart enough to see through all your shenanigans," she said hitting me once more.

We boys scattered for dear life as she hollered, "You boys get back here. I'm not near finished with any of you yet. I'm going to beat you with this here swatter until the darn cows come home."

She stepped off the porch as if to give chase, however by that time the swatter part of the flyswatter had torn apart, all she had left was a piece of wire with tiny shreds of wire on the end.

I stayed out until just before dark, dreading to go into the house knowing what was waiting for me, but to my surprise she was sitting in her favorite chair laughing, kind of twirling a new flyswatter in her hands.

If there is one thing I have learned in my life it's that when things go your way to thank the Lord for that and never, but never, rock the boat, so from that day on I never brought up the love notes again, or should I say what my grandmother called sex notes.

The reason she called them sex notes I didn't find out until the summer of 1960.

Chapter Twenty

The last week before school started up again a tornado did some damage just northeast of town. My mother and grandmother were worried it might have caused some damage to Mr. and Mrs. Hulstine's house. They tried reaching them by phone, however the several times they called, there was no answer.

They asked Charlie and me to walk the couple of miles out to their home to see if they were okay or if they might need help getting things in order if the tornado did any damage to their place.

I didn't dislike the Hulstine's. I just didn't like being around them all that much. Mr. Hulstine was getting up in age. His eyes had long ago started going bad. When it got to the point glasses no longer helped, he ended up getting a seeing eye dog he named Boomer.

It became as normal as breathing to see Boomer leading Mr. Hulstine to the different places around town each day. It looked to people around Verden as if Mr. Hulstine didn't mind all that much losing his eyesight, because he loved Boomer so much.

After only three years, Boomers sight started to fail as well. The veterinarian in Chickasha called it Sudden Acquired Retinal Degeneration, however Mr. Hulstine didn't put much trust in a veterinarian that moonlighted as a pastry chef.

"Must not be much of a vet if he has to moonlight as a pastry chef," he would say to anyone that would listen.

Slowly Boomer got to the point that he couldn't see much better than Mr. Hulstine. People in town learned to move out of the way when they saw the two of them coming. Many times old Boomer led him into the Bank, where Mr. Hulstine, instead of cashing a check or whatever, would ask for a can of green beans or such, thinking he was in the grocery store. Onetime he thought it would be funny to ask for the large economy pack of condoms, thinking he was talking to the Bill Lowtower the druggist. Imagine what Melissa Hicks must have thought when an old man, around eighty or ninety, was standing in front of her cage asking for the economy pack of condoms, or what Mr. Hulstine must have thought when he heard a woman's voice asking him to wait a minute please while she got the manager.

It got to the point Mrs. Hulstine had to keep him and Boomer from going to town. She was deathly afraid that one day old Boomer would walk him into the path of a speeding train.

Keeping him from his daily walks however started to drive the old man into a depression. He no longer had the good appetite he once had. He started getting short with his wife and anyone else that happened along or came to visit him. All he wanted to do was sit in his old rocker, rock back and forth. Boomer however seemed real happy to just lay by the rocker and lick himself, eat when fed, lay back down and lick some more.

It all got too much for Mrs. Hulstine. When he just stopped talking one day, she would ask him something like what he wanted for dinner, he wouldn't even look up toward her voice, just rock.

She was sure that one day she would either wake up finding him dead sitting in his rocker, something she said would drive her into the same depression.

Not wanting that to ever happen, she decided to get him another dog to lead him around town.

She contacted the same people where she got Boomer; unfortunately, they didn't have a dog like Boomer that was ready to be given out as yet.

Mrs. Hulstine told them about the depression her husband had gone in over not being able to go to town and visit his friends and how she was afraid she would find him all dead and stiff in his rocker some morning. She begged them for any help they could give to help her save the life of her husband.

They told her they did have a weenie dog some of the fellows taught to be a Seeing Eye dog during slow times. They said they had no intention of letting it go out in the public, but if she wanted to try to use the weenie dog to save her husband, they were willing to let her try.

Mrs. Hulstine jumped at the chance to use that little weenie dog.

When she got home with Wiener, the name the training center had given him, Wiener took right up with Boomer.

Mrs. Hulstine wanted to let Boomer just lay around the house, but Mr. Hulstine had grown to attached to him They made a heck of a site, walking around town, Wiener out in front, big old Boomer following while Mr. Hulstine held onto the harness attached to Boomer.

Not once did he ask the wrong person for a can of green beans, or say something to Melissa Hick to make her turn as red as a beet run for the manager.

Mrs. Hulstine was an exceptionally nice lady. Everyone in town called her Sister Pam. I asked my grandmother how Sister Pam came up with such a name.

"Well boy, Mrs. Hulstine or Sister Pam as most folks call her now days, was once one of them Catholic nuns. Way I hear it, she turned in her nun costume one morning. She just got up a sister of the Catholic faith around six o'clock in the morning. By eight o'clock she was as normal as you and me, well me anyway," she said, smiling at me.

"Now most people believe nuns quit being nuns because sometime or other when they are locked in prayer like a good nun is suppose to be doing, something snaps in their minds. No one knows what causes it, but something or other snaps," she said, sitting down on the edge of the bed she was making up.

"Some decide they want a family. Others just get tired of so much praying I recon. Other things, I am sure, drives them out of the nunnery, but that wasn't the reason Sister Pam quit. No, sir. Not the reason at all," she said.

"Nope, what caused Sister Pam to shuck her habit was someone took her Saint Christopher medal while she what taking a shower. Can you believe that boy? A thief in a convent! Now I can understand a no-account trying to take something that doesn't belong to them at the five and dime, or Sears or other places like that, because the world is full of no-accounts, but to steal something from a nun while she is just as naked, as naked can be in a convent, boy, that takes some gall," she said.

"You know just as well as I do, as much as I've preached it to you, that the Lord sees and knows everything we do down here. But you can bet if He was to happen to miss something, it wouldn't be something that happened in a convent. I'm sure He keeps an extra special eye on convents," she said, a little anger building in her voice.

"Now don't get me wrong, a nun is just a lady that lives for the Lord, but if in a girl goes into a nunnery with a little kleptomaniac in her heart, well what you have then is a kleptomaniac nun. Course there isn't a lot to steal around a place like that, maybe a cross here and there, or if she wanted to kleptomaniac something big, I figure she could steal that baby Jesus the Catholic's are so grand about putting on the church lawn during Christmas, or one of them bottles of wine the priest used when they were preaching a mass. Course, I'm pretty sure it would be easy enough to spot a drunken nun bonking off the church wall and all," she said, standing up

"When Sister Pam went to the head nun to raise concerns about her medal. She was told to hush up and make no stink about it, however that medal was given to her by her brother before he shipped out to Korea to fight them North Korean fellows. He wasn't in the country no more than a few hours before he stepped on a land mind blowing off four of his toes. They sent him home after that. Said a solider isn't much good trying to fight a war with only a big toe," she continued

"She kept going down to the sister that was running things around there day after day with the same results being for her to hush up. When someone took her picture of Jimmy Stewart that was just too much for her. She went to bed that night one upset sister. When she woke up, she packed her things moved back home. I think she was so upset with the nuns that she started going to the Church of Christ," my grandmother said, laughing

"I was told she Met Mr. Hulstine, one afternoon in Chickasha at the Dairy Queen, when she stopped in to get herself a foot long hotdog, said it was love at first site, but then you got to remember she had been locked up in a convent for a few years so bout any man that would pay any attention to her at all she would have thought she was plum in love. They got married only a couple weeks after they met and moved to Verden to raise a family," she told me.

"They had two kids, a boy that was sure a fine fellow. I think he moved to Phoenix and married a girl from there and started a rest home. Last I heard, it was doing right well. Now their daughter was a different matter altogether. She was so mean, I'm sure she had a hard time getting along with herself. She married some fellow from Edmond. That marriage didn't last long. Apparently she got upset on the way to the motel from the wedding, got out gave the bridegroom a cussing and walked home and filed for a divorce the next day. Since they never made it to the motel, the lawyer got the whole thing annulled," Granny said.

"About six weeks after that, she met a fellow that raised sheep south of Chickasha. They married about three weeks later. This time they made it to the motel. All went well for the two of them for about a month, until she started getting upset and telling him he was spending too much time with the sheep. Myself, I couldn't blame the fellow, as mean as she was. She wouldn't cook or clean and started to gain a lot of weight, so he filed for divorce. Again, she went back home until she met a fellow that was just as mean as she was. After they were married, I was told they moved to Tulsa and got along just fine. Well, if you call getting along fine if you call her getting locked up now and then for domestic abuse just fine," she finished.

When we got to the Hulstine, the storm had missed their property. They gave us a thank you for coming out to check on them along with a glass of lemon aid.

Chapter Twenty-One

The Friday before we boys had to go back to school, we were talking to Mr. Burger at the depot. He was telling us about a family living two miles south of Verder that he figured was a bit touched. My grandmother called just about everyone that she ran into that seemed strange to her, no-accounts. Well, in Mr. Burgers case, everyone he didn't understand or seemed a bit strange to him was touched.

"Did you boys know that Verden has a distinction that no other town in these here United States of America can brag about?" he asked, looking to one another of us.

None of us gave him a verbal no. We just shook our heads no.

"It's a pure wonder none of your parents has said anything about this. Sure, I guess it's nothing big like the Golden Gate Bridge they have over to San Francisco, or them presidents' faces on that mountain up there in South Dakota, but all the same it's a mighty big distinction right here in Verden," he said.

"What is it?" Jake asked before one of us others did.

"Well boys, we have a family living a couple miles north east of Verden that… how should I say this… is a bit touched," he said.

"Dewey and Willie May Doolinger have never gotten along from day one. Day one being the day the two of them hitched up over to Chickasha at the court house," he said, leaning back and crossing his legs, something we boys knew meant he was getting ready to get deep into a story.

"Only thing Willie May brought into the marriage was her clothes and a cat that had no front legs. It had to push it's self around with its two back legs. Dewey made a little wagon-type thing he attached to it, kind of like a small harness. That helped that old cat a tremendous amount getting around. Heck, it wasn't ever able to get up the speed to catch a mouse. If it got to going too fast on that little wagon, it had one heck of a time stopping. Several times it ran smack into the wall or a chair leg. I was told it was trying to catch something or other once, however before it could stop, it slid under the couch and was stuck there several days before the smell gave its location away. That caused a heck of a riff between the two of them. Willie May had it in her mind that the little wagon Dewey made for her cat was nothing more than a device that came from his evil mind to murder her little cat, Scooter," Mr. Burger said.

"The other thing she brought into the marriage was her prize milk cow that she raised from the day it was born. She loved that cow and would talk to it same as we are talking here. Dewey hated the cow. He said it took his wife away from him and her chores around the house too much, but he wasn't about to tell her that, especially after the death of Sscooter," he said, leaning forward.

"Dewey thought Willie May might like it if he would lead the cow down to one of the many ponds he had to let it walk out into the water and cool off from the scorching sun. When the cow waded out a little ways into the water, unbeknown to the cow as well as Dewey, it waded right smack into a swarm of water moccasins. People said it got bit by the cottonmouth snakes so many times, a person would be hard-pressed to find a spot on one of its four legs that didn't have a bite spot on it," he said, looking from one to the other of us.

"Wow, what happened then?" Bruce asked.

"That cow was lucky enough to get out of the water, but it no more than got on dry land than it collapsed just a few feet from the water. It lay there bellowing something purely awful,. Willie May was doing dishes, looking out the kitchen window when she saw the cow lying on its side. Dewey was dancing around hollering something. Being out of ear shot, she couldn't tell what Dewey was hollering. She dropped the plate she was drying. It shattering into a thousand pieces hitting the tile floor," he said.

"Willie May got to the cow and Dewey just in time to watch her prize cow bellow it's last time in this lifetime. Willie May came apart like one of them watches they give away at the fair. I was told if she had had a gun or knife with her she would have murdered her husband pure and simple. Killed him right there on the spot," Mr. Burger said, standing up stretching.

"Willie May was so upset about the cow, she made Dewey sleep in the tack room in the barn. She would make breakfast and have it on the table at six in the morning. She let Dewey in for ten minutes, and ten minutes only, to eat. At six o'clock in the evening, she would sit dinner on the table and let him back in for one hour to eat and take a shower if he thought he might need one. All that hour, she would sit in their bedroom singing Red River Valley, and believe me that woman couldn't sing. Fact is, she couldn't carry a tune in a full size dump truck. She only sang the song to irritate the heck out of Dewey," he said.

"Dewey was at his wits end trying to figure out how to get back in the good graces of Willie May, however everything he thought might work completely flopped on him. He bought roses from the florist in Chickasha leaving them on the table after he ate. The next morning they were mixed in with his scrambled eggs and sausage. Three of four of them were floating around in his coffee. He bought her a new blue dress with white spots from Sears in Chickasha. The only problem with the size he was looking at, was extra small. After looking for a long time, he finally found one that he thought was the correct size. It turned out to be wrong because it was a double triple X which was about six sizes too large for her. The next evening, the dress had been cut down the side and made into a table cloth that more than covered the table his burnt hamburger steak was sitting on," Mr. Burger said, sitting back down.

"One afternoon, about three weeks after the dress incident, he was at Wards in Chickasha again when he noticed a young couple looking over a washing machine. It looked to him as if the girl was glowing walking around the machine. I wasn't there, but I can imagine what went through his head watching the young girl. I believe Dewey figured that if he bought Willie May one of those machines, she would have to forgive him for the cat and her stupid cow," he said, smiling.

"When the machine was delivered, Willie May got so excited that she would no longer have to use the scrub board to get the clothes clean, she did forgive Dewey. She let him come back into his house the very same day. She even cooked him his favorite dinner that night, pinto beans with fried potatoes. After supper Dewey went about hooking up the washer. When it was all ready, Willie May loaded it with a load of whites. Together they stood arm in arm watching it as it washed the clothes. Once it completed its washing cycle, all that was left to do was run the clothes through the wringer on top of the machine, squeezing the water out good enough to hang the clothes on the clothesline. Dewey was watching Willie May running the things through the ringer and he had to smile at her excitement because he knew his life was going to change for the better, all because he was smart enough to buy her that washer," Mr. Burger said, leaning forward and placing his elbows on the desk.

"He snapped back to reality when he heard Willie May let out a loud a piercing scream. Moving next to her, it looked as if she had bent over to get a t-shirt out of the washer and when she straightened up, her being a well-endowed woman, her left breast touched the bottom roller of the two rollers, and it was pulling her left breast into the wringer. In fact, it was pulling all of her into the thing, squeezing her breast almost flat. Dewey not knowing what to do, since he knew nothing about washing machines, unplugged it, hoping he was in time to save his wife's breast from being pulled completely off. All Willie May could do was scream for help. Dewey ran to the phone calling the volunteer fire department, the Highway Patrol, even the ambulance from Chickasha as well as Anadarko," Mr. Burger said, getting a kick out of his own story.

"When all the emergency people arrived, several of the men just stood around, never having seen anything like a woman with her left breast in a washing machine wringer. When the highway patrol trooper arrived, he walked straight over to the machine turned the little black knob on top of the wringer releasing the two rollers and freeing Willie May. The trooper used his hand held radio and called his dispatcher, explaining all was clear and that he helped free a lady with her tit in a wringer. He said that before he thought about what he was saying. Everyone in the room but Willie May broke out in laughter. It didn't take long until that was a phrase used all over town, then all over Oklahoma. Now I'm told, it is used all around the world. When someone is caught doing something wrong, or in trouble, it is known as they got their tit in a wringer," he said.

"What happen to the Doolingers?" Jake asked.

"Well, I'm told that Willie May filed for divorce the very next day, using the grounds her husband was trying to drive her crazy. Dewey still lives in the same house, has the same washing machine, said he would never get married again even if the woman that wanted to marry him had hundred dollar bills shooting out her backside every few minutes," he said.

Chapter Twenty-Two

I suppose one of the last things I got into that summer before school started, was the day my grandmother sent me to town to pay the grocery bill. Back in 1959, the grocer had no problem letting a family charge whatever they needed to tide them over until their Social Security check came in around the first of each month.

My grandmother hated it called Social Security. She called it, and made me as well as everyone else around her, call it her no-account check. She said she received that check once a month for having to put up with all the no-accounts around town. Said it wasn't near enough but then the no-accounts living in Washington kept most of the money for themselves, so she felt darn lucky to get what she got.

One of my chores each month was to make sure that bill was paid, if the need be. I had to remind my grandmother about that bill each day from the first of the month until her check came and it got paid.

Gary and I were on our way to the store that morning with the twenty-two dollars and sixty-eight cents to pay the bill, when we ran into Cucumber Bill.

Cucumber Bill lived in a oneroom house, a block east of the welding shop. When I say a one room house, I meant just that. He lived in a house that only had one room, no kitchen, no bathroom, just the one bedroom.

When he needed to go to the bathroom, since his house was more or less out of view of just about everything in town, Bill just stacked up two are three tires and tied them together with a couple of pieces of rope. The tires made a mighty fine restroom he would tell people if they happen to ask. People said once the smell would get to be too much, he would head to the dump and pick up new tires. When someone happened to see him rolling a tire down Main Street, they knew old Cucumber was building a new bathroom.

Cucumber got the name Cucumber Bill because of his temper. He would get mad at a person at the drop of a hat. Mr. Burger said one Sunday morning, Cucumber was sitting in the First Baptist Church about middle ways holding his Bible and taking in everything the preacher had to say, when all of a sudden he stood up and pulled a cucumber out of his coat pocket and chunked it at the preacher.

Before Mr. Burger and a couple other men could grab a hold of him, he chunked three or four more cucumbers at the preacher, one hitting Mr. Patillo, who was one of the deacons standing off to the side of the preacher holding several of them plates they pass around to collect everyone's ten percent. Mr. Burger said it near broke Mr. Patillo's nose when it hit him. Made him drop the four plates he was holding by the feet of Mr. Boyer, who was sleeping like a new born baby. People said when those plates hit the floor, it near caused Mr. Boyer to go smooth into one of them cardiac arrests. They had to call the ambulance from Chickasha over to check him out.

Only reason cucumber was mad, he happened to check his pocket watch and he had seen it was three minutes past noon. He said the preacher spent most all the hour talking about how people wasn't giving enough to the church and that the good Lord above was about to come down and do just a whole bunch of smiting, cleaning house on all the sinners sitting in front of him that was holding back on their ten percent.

Mr. Burger said Cucumber thought with all that ten percent talk, a fellow wasn't getting his spiritual needs met, so he started chunking cucumber at the preacher. Whenever Bill got mad, which was most of the time, he would throw cucumbers at whoever he was mad at. He always carried a bag full of cucumbers with him wherever he went.

When Les Waller shot himself climbing through a fence Dove hunting, Cucumber Bill was waiting outside the funeral home when they brought the coffin out to head to the graveyard. Soon as Les was loaded up in the back of that hearse, Bill went to throwing cucumbers' at it and chasing it several blocks still throwing cucumbers. Mr. Burger figured he would have run all the way to the cemetery if he hadn't ran out of cucumbers first.

Someone asked him why he did that to poor old Mr. Waller. He told them it was because Mr. Waller was a bootlegger and they just left it at that, not wanting to get Cucumber Bill mad at them.

That morning as Gary and I walked by him, he had his head down so I couldn't tell for sure, but it looked like he had been crying.

"What's wrong?" I asked him.

"Hi Gary, Sonny. It's the mayor and them cronies he has. They tell me my place stinks and that I got to do something about it or they will condemn it and make me move," he answered.

"Can they do that?" I asked.

"I sure reckon they can. It says right here on this paper if'n I don't have her cleaned up in thirty days they'll have the sheriff come throw me out on the street," he said, holding the paper out for us to look at.

"Well, all you have to do is fix the place up somewhat," Gary said.

"I did. Come let me show you," he said, leading us toward his house.

"See," he said pointing to the back of the house.

What he had done was place pieces of plywood over the tires to control the smell, but when you have twenty or more tires stacked up that were used as bathrooms over the years, pieces of thin plywood doesn't even come close to controlling the smell they put out.

We boys could dig a hole to help him shove that stuff in, and cover it up. Math wasn't either Gary or my best subject, but we figured with all five of us digging and Cucumber helping, it would take a couple hours each day, and with going to school during the day, it would take about two years, so that was out since he only had thirty days to get everything cleaned up.

As much as we boys liked to help people and as hard as we two thought, we could come up with nothing.

Gary thought we might go borrow one of the bulldozers parked east of town that had been used to build roads to and from oilfield locations.

I didn't think much of that idea because none of us had ever been on a bulldozer. In fact, I was pretty sure no one in our little group had the first idea how to even start the thing. I wondered what kind of trouble we would get into driving a bulldozer to Cucumber's house in order to try to dig a hole big enough to push all the tires he used as restrooms into.

No, we decided against that right off the bat. If we destroyed something with a bulldozer, they would put us under the jail.

"I'm sorry Bill, I don't know what to do to help you," I said, putting my hand on his shoulder.

"It's okay, boys. I'll just move in with Jim and Eden until I can find me another place to live," he said, taking a cucumber out of his pocket.

I sure hoped we hadn't gotten him mad and him fixing to start throwing them at us. Instead, he just took a bite out of the thing.

His brother Jim lived south of town, close to where all the Mennonite farms started. Before Jim married his wife, Eden, she was a member of the Mennonite Church. He met her by a quirk of circumstances. I was told by Mr. Finchmoore that Jim was out hunting arrowheads a couple of days after his eighteenth birthday. Back then you could find arrowheads just about anywhere around the area. We figured it was because Anadarko was known as the Indian capital of the world.

Once you found an arrowhead, you could take it to the Indian museum in Anadarko and sell it to them from five to ten cents, according to what condition it happened to be in.

One with the point broken off, or the piece missing, you might get only a nickel, but one that was intact would easily bring a dime.

Then the Museum would, in return, put them in a little wicker basket and sell them for around a quarter to people that visited the museum.

Jim had become friends with Mr. Wantland, a Mennonite farmer. One afternoon while looking for arrowheads, Jim saw Mr. Wantland plowing up a field with his donkey. Jim waited until he came back around to where he was standing.

When Mr. Wantland came around, Jim asked him if it would be okay if he tried to find arrowheads in his freshly plowed field.

"Sure Jim. You have at it," he said, smiling at Jim

As Jim climbed through the fence, Mr. Wantland said, "My daughter Eden will be bringing out some lemonade pretty soon. Better have some."

Jim noticed Eden as she walked up the road carrying the pitcher of lemonade. Mr. Wantland noticed Jim looking down the road and was pretty sure he knew what Jim was looking at. Joining Jim, the two stood watching Eden approaching.

When Eden reached them, Jim was dumbfounded. Apparently, he had never seen a girl as pretty as Eden even with the long blue plaid dress she was wearing, along with the white bonnet she had on her head covering her blond hair.

Jim not being a Mennonite, he wasn't real sure how to talk to Mr. Wantland, or to Eden for that matter. He wasn't even sure if he was supposed to talk to her, her being not married and such.

He was so interested in her, he said without thinking, "Mr. Wantland, I know you Mennonites put great store in your traditions, not having any televisions in your houses, no radios in your cars, and that you have milk cows always hanging around and such."

Mr. Wantland and Eden looked at Jim as if the sun might have gotten to him all of a sudden. They thought that maybe he became disorientated, being out in the direct sun and not being used to it or its effects.

All Mr. Wantland could answer was, "What… what's that you're saying Jim?"

"Well it's about your daughter. I know you wouldn't let a non-Mennonite ever date her, because you people have a standard you have to keep up with. But sir, if you were to let me come calling on Eden, well sir, just as soon as I can afford to buy a car, I will tear the radio antenna right off it and I'll pull the radio out, and even take the white wall tires off it, well, if it comes with white wall tires that is. And to top that all off sir, I will buy myself a milk cow soon as I find enough arrowheads." Jim said to Mr. Wantland

Eden started to laugh, laughing so hard she had to sit down.

Mr. Wantland looked as if someone just shot him. He wasn't mad, and he didn't think it funny. He was confused. Being a Mennonite all his life, he had no idea what to say to Jim. He knew Jim probably meant every word he just said, so he really didn't want to hurt the boy's feelings.

"Well Jim, it's not so much traditions. It's more of how we believe, if you must. It's our religion and how we interpret the Bible," Mr. Wantland said, looking down at Eden laughing.

"Well sir, I have me a Bible. I know all about Bible stuff. I know about that big flood they had over there somewhere in England or Spain and about that young fellow chunking that rock killing that big fellow. I know about how that old fellow lead them three or four hundred people out of that country, cause of all the plagues going on around there. And yes, I know how they crucified the Lord on a cross between I believe, a burglar and the other fellow, but I'm not real sure what the other feller did. More than likely or not, he was an armed robber or such," Jim said

Hearing Jim explaining the Bible like he was, got Eden laughing even harder, if that was possible. Tears were running down her cheeks from laughing so hard.

"Well Jim, I am sorry, but as Mennonites, we like our children to marry within the faith," he said.

"Well if I were to become a Mennonite, could I come calling then?" Jim asked.

Hearing that, Eden stopped laughing as she realized Jim was really bent on courting her.

To shut Jim up, he told him that if indeed he did become a Mennonite, he would let him court her.

Eden just stood back up smiling, then headed back toward the house.

With that discussion over, Mr. Wantland went back to plowing and Jim continued walking around the field looking for arrowheads, with a big smile on his face.

That next Sunday, Mr. Wantland was standing around before church telling the other men and a couple of young boys about Jim and about everything Jim had to say. They all seemed to be getting a good laugh out of it, when up walked Jim wearing a pair of jeans that had been cut off, a pair of sandals, and a t-shirt that said "Fly the friendly skies of Japan," with the picture of a B-29 bomber dropping bombs.

Before Mr. Wantland could run interference or stop him, Jim walked into the church as if he had been coming there since birth. Seeing Eden sitting with a bunch of girls in the front, he walked down to the pew she was sitting in and excused himself as he started moving down the pew to sit next to her. He had no clue that in that church, unmarried girls sit on the right in front while the unmarried boys sit on the other side, up front. The married women sit behind the girl. The married men sit behind the boys. In spite of their traditions, there sat Jim, right smack in the middle of the unmarried girls.

"How's it going?" he asked Eden, sitting down next to her.

"You can't sit here," she whispered back.

"No worries. No one will even notice me," he answered

Looking around the church, she could see every eye in the place was now trained on her and Jim.

After church, Mr. Wantland took Jim aside and tried to explain to him about how things worked in church. It did stop Jim from sitting next to Eden from then on, and he did start wearing full pants with a shirt with a collar, but Mr. Wantland didn't sway him one bit from going to church, or his dream of courting Eden.

This went on for an entire year, until one evening Eden didn't show up for supper. That was something that was unheard of in the Mennonite community. Every one of the Mennonites went out hunting Eden. Some of them were sure something really bad must have happened to her. Some people even believed she must have been murdered in some sick despicable manner, while others figured things like she just got plum tired of wearing them long dresses. Others said it was the bonnet caused her to run away. They figured it was more than likely that she caught herself a ride and headed to New York City, or someplace up around there.

They hunted for several days or until church that next Sunday morning. When Jim didn't show up, Mr. Wantland got to figuring. Jim either heard that Eden was missing, then decided what the heck no need to go if she wasn't going to be there. But the more he thought about it, he figured those two kids might just be up to no good.

After church he walked over to the little house that Jim bought a mile or so from the church. Hiding in some tall grass in back of the house, he waited, hoping his thoughts might be wrong.

After waiting for about an hour in the grass, he decided he must be wrong, when out came Jim carrying a garden hoe. Mr. Wantland just figured he was going to hoe the weeds out of his pitiful looking garden.

"Bring in a couple of tomatoes, if there are any ready to pick." A voice came from the house.

That voice he knew very well. He should. He had been feeding it, clothing it, loving it for the last eighteen years.

Right behind the voice stepped Eden onto the back steps.

"Eden," he hollered at her.

You would have thought someone just pulled the shower curtain back, catching her naked, the expression on her face. First it was confusion, followed by fear that turned into shame.

Jim came running when he heard Mr. Wantland's voice.

"Sir, we are sorry about this, but we fell smooth in love, meeting and talking every church day. We knew you would never let me court her, much less marry her, even if I bought myself one of them milk cows, no matter what I did not being a Mennonite and all," Jim said in a pleading voice.

"Sneaking off caused so much worry among our Church brethren and so many nights your poor mother spent sleepless and crying over you," he said looking at his daughter.

"Eden, I might forgive all that, because you two are so young and I hate to say it, stupid, but to live together in sin, that is something I just can't abide by after all I have tried to teach you about the Bible," he said looking at them both.

"But Father, there is no sin here. I would never do that to you and mother, never. When Jim and I left, we caught a ride and went down to Wichita Falls Texas where we got married by a Justice of Peace," she said, tears starting to run down her cheeks.

"I wished I could tell you all went well after he found out those two youngsters were married, but being a good Mennonite, he had to shun Eden, and all the other Mennonite folks shunned her, too," Mr. Finchmoore said, as he told us the story.

"Jim and Eden still live in the same house. Jim made a go of the farm and bought a car. His word was good. He took the radio out, and ripped off the antenna, even bought a couple of milk cows," he told us.

"No matter what Jim did, her father wouldn't have anything more to do with his daughter, even when her two twin boys were born," Mr. Finchmoore said.

"But as for Bill living with them until he finds another place, well Eden and Jim love Bill, but whenever Bill happens to see a Mennonite, he goes to chucking cucumbers at them, and boys that is sure not a good way to bring a father and daughter back together.

"Time will tell. Time will tell," he said

Bill moved in with his brother and promised to not chunk cucumbers anymore at Mennonites, which lasted about one day.

We boys started back to school a few days after that, looking for the summer of 1960, wondering what the 60s would bring.

THE END

ABOUT THE AUTHOR

R. J. was born in Oklahoma City, Oklahoma, in 1946. He attended no less than a dozen elementary schools as his family traveled working with the pipeline up until the fourth grade, then finally settling in Chickasha, Oklahoma. R.J. graduated in 1965. After graduating he spent four years in the U.S. Navy. After leaving Uncle Sam he worked his way up in construction to the position of civil superintendent, the field he still works in today.

R.J. and his wife, Marsha, collectively have two daughters, one son and two grandchildren. Writing is R.J.'s golf! When others head off to the greens, R.J. enjoys writing. He has written several different types of novels throughout the years from suspense to horror. However he believes writing humor is what he enjoys the most.

His first installment in The Boys Series, The Boys of '58 was released in 2011. Readers can also look forward to The Boys of '60 and more.

R.J. will tell you he is proud to be a card holder and a member by blood of the Choctaw Nation of Oklahoma.

He hopes to retire very soon and dedicate all his free time to his passion for writing.